DR. SUNSHINE

DR. SUNSHINE

A NOVEL

LEO WOLF

TEN SPEED PRESS
BERKELEY, CALIFORNIA

1⊜

TEN SPEED PRESS
P.O. Box 7123
Berkeley, California 94707

Cover design by Fifth Street Design
Book design by Ralph Fowler

Library of Congress Cataloging-in-Publication Data
Wolf, Leo.
    Dr. Sunshine : a novel / Leo Wolf.
       p.   cm.
    ISBN 0-89815-526-6
    I. Title.
PS3562.04876D7   1993   92-34863
813'.54—dc20   CIP

FIRST PRINTING 1993
1 2 3 4 5 — 97 96 95 94 93

DR. SUNSHINE

1

Dr. Hillel Sunshine fell in love at least three times a day. In 1971—the Chinese Year of the Pig—he had his first extramarital affair. In 1972—the Year of the Rat—he was head over heels (to cite one of many positions) in love (to cite one of several self-deceptions) with dozens of women.

In 1976—the Year of the Dragon—he consulted his horoscope and set out to have an affair, inside of twelve months, with "every woman under the sun," beginning with an Aries and ending with a Pisces. His desire to pluck, as it were, from the zodiac one lovely lady born under each of the sun signs was a desperate effort to bring order out of his chaotic love life—a love life that included fourteen years of marriage to the same woman.

A tortured soul in a pleasured body, he reasoned that if he could limit his dalliance to one woman a month for a year, he could kick his addiction to sex and return to his first love, the practice of internal medicine—and to his second, his family. For better or for worse, in sickness and in health, Dr. Sunshine was primarily a physician, secondarily a married man, and terminally, a lover.

It was time to stop. Increasing numbers of doctors who slept with their patients were being sued for malpractice. So far he had been incredibly careful—and lucky. Some lawyers were predicting that this type of professional hanky-panky would someday become a criminal offense—for doctors, not lawyers. It was time to stop.

Sexually transmitted diseases were proliferating and proving more difficult to treat. It was time to stop.

But how? He knew he couldn't quit suddenly without failing. ("How can you go from hot chicks to cold turkey?" he rhetorically asked his psychiatrist.) In the end, he decided to cut his dose to one affair each month for a year—his own Twelve-Step program, as he called it—then get out for good.

By 1977—the Year of the Snake—the worm had turned. Dr. Sunshine was practicing the best medicine of his career, he was once more monogamous, and the last twelve women he had loved and left were fond and fading memories.

With the help of a psychiatrist, Dr. Sunshine had finally laid his sexual demons to rest. He could not have known that his sexual demons had similar plans for him.

2 THURSDAY, MARCH 23, 1978
10:00 P.M. BERKELEY, CALIFORNIA

The twelve naked women lay on their backs in a circle on the dark blue Karistan rug. All former lovers of Dr. Sunshine, they were the spokes in a living astrological wheel, from redheaded Aries counterclockwise to ash-blonde Pisces. Their painted toenails formed a scarlet rosette at the center of the wheel; their outstretched arms defined its circumference. A three-hundred-watt bulb in a ceiling lamp bathed their supine bodies in warm, bright rays of ultraviolet light. "Doctored sunshine," thought their guru, as he lay back on his Eames lounger and basked in the light. With pride, he regarded the dazzling reflection of his heavenly wheel in the mirrored ceiling.

The light caught the women's lustrous hair to fashion a multihued corona around the luminous circle of their half-drugged bodies. "If not a Busby Berkeley creation, then at least a Berkeley one," thought the guru, staring up entranced at the ring of bright women.

The fair-skinned, blue-eyed guru was dressed in a black, understated version of an SS colonel's uniform (no swastikas or decorations, just the simple white death's-head above the visor of the hat). He stood up and began pacing the perimeter of the circle. In a loud, imperious voice that would have commanded the unflinching attention of seven thousand men on a parade ground, he shouted, "Kleenex!" The twelve unclad women, flaked out on the floor, stared unblinking into the light.

"Kleenex!" he repeated. "Dr. Sunshine used you like Kleenex! He sneezed into you—then tossed you away. Yes, sneezed! Poked a fleshy protuberance into your soft tissues, had his snotty spasm, and then *dropped* you. Achoo! Achoo! . . . *Gesundheit* and good-bye. Is that any way to treat a lady?"

In perfect unison, the somnolent women languidly chorused, "No way, Werner."

The black-booted guru halted, placed his hands on his hips, and glared down at his circle. "Tomorrow night you will avenge all women who have ever been *used* by men. You will remind the *world* that what men call 'casual sex' can break a woman's *heart*. Tomorrow night, each of you will show Dr. Sunshine that an Angel of Death is looking for more than a one-night stand."

The guru turned a rheostat. The overhead light began to dim. "And now," he said, raising his right arm in a stiff salute, "Sun signs, rise! Sunshine dies!"

As the room darkened, the women came fully awake and sat up. Instinctively seeking the last glimmerings of light, they stared into the gas-blue eyes of Werner von Mundt.

3   FRIDAY, MARCH 24, 1978
5:50 P.M. BERKELEY

ARIES
Take heart, Ari Baby. Tonight you must try for meaningful contact with loved one. Give it your best shot.

Pale fingers of light from the setting sun caressed the hard phallic contours of the Polish antitank gun. The incongruity of such a military piece mounted on a grassy knoll at the western edge of the U.C. Berkeley campus was not lost on passing motorists. One after the other, each driver's bearded head jerked to the right. Glittery eyes blinked at the weapon through tinted glasses, then turned forward to glower at the rear end of the Volkswagen ahead.

A panzer division of light-blue, vintage Beetles moved north at last light to the hill-climbing roads off Oxford Street, their drivers dismissing the field gun as an ROTC prop, or a fraternity prank, or an irksome hallucination former users of LSD are wont to have from time to time.

"Oh, shit!"

Crouched behind the gun, the petite redhead in Levi's and a white tank top had just snagged one of her Lee Press-On nails on the breechblock. The plastic fingernail lay scarlet in the dark grass; it was the first casualty the 47-mm Poczisk had inflicted in the thirty-nine years since Von Kluge's Fourth Army had overrun its position. Within minutes, if all went well, the Poczisk would destroy its first German vehicle.

Fingering the stump of her amputated nail, the fetching redhead leaned forward and squinted through the cross-haired sight on the gun barrel. Closely, she beheld another Beetle, another beard—wrong German car, wrong Jewish face.

"Goddam you, Sunshine," she thought, "step on it!" She straightened up and scanned the streets and sidewalks below her.

Her darting green eyes pinpointed her eleven comrades moving swiftly up Oxford to their stations. She glanced at her watch: 5:57 P.M. For luck, she rubbed the Aries pendant hanging like a silvery moon above her alpine breasts. She felt her anger subside.

Soon, Dr. Sunshine's light-green Mercedes would pull away from the stop sign at the corner of University Avenue and Oxford, directly below her. Through narrow, shell-pink nostrils, she inhaled slowly, savoring the seminal scent of newly oiled gunmetal.

It would be like shooting a duck in a crock pot.

4 FRIDAY, MARCH 24, 1978
6:00 P.M. BERKELEY

VIRGO

Plan a quiet evening at home, Virg. Old acquaintances
may pose a threat to domesticity.

The luminous numerals of 6:00 P.M. imprinted themselves on digital watches all over Berkeley—6:00 P.M: for psychiatrists, the tremulous moment between work and play. The moment when hundreds of bearded analysts, wearing festival shirts of coarse fibers woven in Guatemalan villages, spring to their sandaled feet and embrace their last tall blonde patients of the day. For, after all, in the final analysis, what is more therapeutic than a hug? In the final analysis, what,

Freud asked, did women really want? Did his own modesty forbid the answer: A short, bearded Jew, perhaps?

In a two-story stucco building on Prince Street, Dr. Hillel Sunshine, a tall, clean-shaven, forty-three-year-old internist, propelled himself down the taupe-carpeted hallway of his office. As usual, the internist was running late. There would be no blonde patient for Dr. Sunshine to hug at 6:00 P.M. (His fate was not to be an analyst, but to need one.)

Just over six feet tall, this Jewish American Prince was crowned with a fullish head of curly, light-brown hair silvering at the temples. An escapee from the golden ghetto of suburban Pittsburgh, he confronted disease in beige-tinted aviator glasses and a six-hundred-dollar three-piece suit.

At the first sight of his undraped body on their honeymoon in Venice, his wife (a student of the Italian masters) had exclaimed, "Michelangelo's *David*! Joe DiMaggio's *bat*!" Fully clothed and holding forth at, say, a hospital staff party, he was a handsome version, according to his wife, of what you'd get if you stood Dustin Hoffman on Mel Brooks's shoulders—a tall, Jewish professional with an intense demeanor and a gut-level sense of humor.

Before Dr. Sunshine's working day was done, he had yet to see Morris Sappersteen and Hattie Jackson. Then, to please his wife, he was due home for dinner by 6:30.

He threw open the door of his first examining room and unleashed the full power of the Sunshine smile—a glad-to-see-you-I'm-competent-to-meet-your-needs-and-if-you-tell-me-I'm-looking-marvelous-I-won't-hold-it-against-you smile. It was a smile wasted on an empty room. In her haste to leave at 5:30 on the tick, his nurse had failed to tell him that Mr. Sappersteen had called at the last minute to cancel. ("Nurse, I can't make it in today. I'm too sick to see the doctor.")

In the empty room, Dr. Sunshine's smile fell in ruins, leaving a pale, stubbled, slack-jawed face only a mother and two thousand female patients could love. He removed Mr. Sappersteen's chart from the wooden rack screwed to the door and tossed it on top of a filing cabinet. Then he thundered down the hallway to his third examining room where his laboriously reconstructed smile found a 212-pound target.

"Hi, Hattie. It's good to see you."

"Oh, Dr. Sunshine," cried Mrs. Jackson. "You look beautiful!"

5 FRIDAY, MARCH 24, 1978
7:05 A.M. BERKELEY

Dr. Sunshine was losing the momentum he had gained since snapping awake at 7:00 A.M. He started from his nymph-haunted sleep in his large Spanish Colonial high in the verdant hills of Berkeley. A cool breeze poured through an open side window, bearing the distant roar of commuter traffic and the vestigial scent of nocturnal skunk warfare. The sudden thrilling notes of Gershwin, the Sunshines' resident mockingbird, flooded the room with his latest improvisation for his master's approval. To clear his nostrils, Dr. Sunshine turned to sniff the faint, warm, vaporous scent of Je Revien at the nape of his wife's neck.

He sat up on his side of their love-tossed bed and gazed out the picture window. The indigo bowl of San Francisco Bay lay one thousand feet below him (a panoramic bay view—Dr. and Mrs. Sunshine's most treasured possession). Through the soft morning light, he looked across the bay at the white skyline of San Francisco, the burnt-orange Golden Gate Bridge, the purple bulk of Mt. Tam, the bottle-green hills of Marin County.

As he stared at Marin, he reflected that at forty-three he was almost old enough to die of natural causes. Deciding he was working too hard, he resolved to quit at fifty. He imagined his obituary: "In his middle years, Dr. Sunshine retired from the private practice of medicine in Berkeley and founded a halfway house in Marin for intellectually challenged blondes."

He dismissed this thought and turned to kiss the gleaming shoulder of Gloria Goldbloom-Sunshine, his olive-skinned, chestnut-haired wife. (No Nordic numbskull this one!) The rhythmic rise and fall of her ample breasts under the percale sheet assured him that she had not died in the night. He thanked God.

He stood up and followed the morning erection of Poindexter, his phallus, into the bathroom. (Having been born in 1935 A.D.—After Disney—Dr. Sunshine had a tendency to anthropomorphize wild animals. He had named his phallus Poindexter, of course, for its tendency to point, when aroused, to the right.)

Emerging from the bathroom, he entered his den and pedaled twenty sweaty minutes on a Schwinn XR-5. He panted as he scanned *The New England Journal of Medicine* propped up on a rack bolted to the handlebars. At the same time he listened to Mozart's Flute and Harp Concerto on KDFC.

When the bell on his Schwinn finally tolled, he dismounted like Errol Flynn from his stallion in *The Charge of the Light Brigade* (or so he liked to think). After pocketing his two trusty talismans, a frayed, pink rabbit's foot and his Swiss Army knife, he descended to the downstairs bathroom, where he showered hot and hard under his Water Pic Cyclo Massage.

While drying off, he heard a distinctly alien belch erupt from the kitchen. He froze. He knew intimately every sound capable of emanating from each member of his family and *this was something else, from someone else.* He grabbed his Swiss Army knife. Legally blind without his glasses, and naked as a jaybird, he charged into the kitchen shouting, "GET OUT OF HERE YOU MOTHERFUCKER OR I'LL KILL YOU!" Myopically he confronted a middle-aged black woman in a white uniform who let out a whoop of terror. He suddenly remembered that his wife had hired a new housekeeper. Mumbling an apology, he turned his back on the stricken, instantly *former* employee, and retreated to the bathroom, where he collapsed on the commode in a fit of embarrassment and hilarity. Another battle won by his Swiss Army knife, he noted, snapping the blade shut.

He finished drying off, then shaved with his London brush of finest badger tail. After patting his face, torso, and Poindexter with Lagerfeld cologne, he tiptoed upstairs where his family, miraculously, was still asleep. He dressed quickly, tying a perfect Windsor knot in his red, Italian silk tie and slipped himself into a dove-gray suit of three pieces. After an approving glance in the full-length mirror, he squeaked down the hall in mirrored-polished black oxfords to give their sleeping twins, Jonathan and Michael, five seconds each of a father's loving gaze. He thanked God two more times.

At 7:42 A.M., Dr. Sunshine drove his newly washed and polished, light-green Mercedes 450 SEL down the corkscrew of Shasta Road in low gear. From his four Blaupunkt speakers poured Mozart's

Divertimento in D to which he kept time by twanging Poindexter, using his right index finger as though playing a Jew's harp. Through tinted aviator glasses, his quick brown eyes devoured storybook gardens on his left and Technicolor bay views on his right. He loved starting each day replete—his wallet full of twenties, his tank full of gas, his ears full of Mozart, his eyes full of bay views and rose blossoms. The only thing running on empty was his stomach.

Within seven minutes of leaving home, he had found a seat at an empty table in Fat Albert's Grill. He took in the aroma of fried bacon, the white ceramic pitchers heavy with cream, the water in the Silex at a rolling boil, and the lonely, nubile grad students bent over Proust and croissants.

For his Friday morning "prayer breakfast," he ordered two eggs over easy, crisp bacon, home fries, nine-grain toast, and coffee. Fervently, he closed his eyes and prayed that the bacon would be crisp and the eggs soft. Reconnoitering the tables for someone to ogle until his food arrived, he chose a young woman reading by the window, the sun backlighting her honey-blonde hair. Twelve minutes later, he smiled up at the waitress serving him his answered prayers. He peppered his eggs black.

Stomach sated, brakes squealing, he pulled into the parking lot of Bay Vista Convalescent Hospital at 8:25 A.M. to pay his dreaded monthly visit, a month late, to Jacob Krantzler. He opened the carpeted trunk of his Mercedes and grabbed his doctor's bag, the lineal descendent of the black leather case of women's glove samples his father had schlepped out of Chevrolets for thirty years.

Charging down the yellow linoleum corridor of the nursing home, he stepped squarely into a puddle of urine. He cursed with abandon as he negotiated a five-foot glissade past the open door of Emma Goldfarb's room, startling her awake from a twelve-year torpor. (Mrs. Goldfarb envisioned the spitting image of her husband, Max, who had died forty years before, slide by her open door. Just like Max to be hot under the collar about something and not even give her the time of day, she thought.)

Back on dry linoleum, Dr. Sunshine traced the source of urine to a leaky plastic bag strapped to the side of Jacob Krantzler's wheelchair, which was inching down the hall up ahead. This was Krantzler's method, he surmised, of destroying would-be attackers from the rear—learned, no doubt, from watching James Bond reruns on the Magnavox in the dayroom.

Dr. Sunshine bestowed his million-dollar smile and forty-dollar handshake on Mr. Jacob Krantzler, who farted cordially in response. He then leaned down to shout into the elderly patient's better ear, "HOW'S IT GOING, JAKE?"

Krantzler shot a left hook to Sunshine's jaw, knocking off the doctor's glasses. While Sunshine took the mandatory eight count, he resolved never to lead with his chin against Kid Krantzler again. Clamping on his stethoscope, he listened briefly to Krantzler's heart and lungs, then felt the old man's neck.

In Krantzler's chart, he wrote an order for a blood T3 by RIA to confirm his suspicion that the patient had developed thyrotoxicosis (warm, trembling hands, rapid resting pulse, unblinking gaze, lightning left hook).

Deeply inhaling the relatively fresh air outside the nursing home, he leaped into his getaway car and was soon gunning to 45 mph down Grove Street. At the corner of Derby, he suddenly braked for a quadriplegic young woman in a powered wheelchair who was about to enter the crosswalk. Recognizing her as one of the patients he treated at the Berkeley Free Clinic, he touched his hand to his lips and blew her a kiss. Unable to raise her arm, she returned his airborne hello with a dazzling smile and a saucy wink.

At 9:03 A.M., he parked his gleaming Mercedes in the garage below his office. With his head bowed to avoid eye contact with lurking drug company reps, he briskly walked the half-block to Alta Bates Hospital. He zipped through his acute hospital rounds. He confronted five patients in fourteen minutes—three elective handshakes and two emergency thigh squeezes—all patients cheered by his appearance, all doing well.

He raced back to his office, up two flights of stairs, two at a time. "Good morning, sweetheart!" he enthused to Mrs. Katz, his gray-haired, long-suffering nurse, who cut him dead for being twenty minutes late. Stepping into his immaculate office bathroom, he combed the morning breeze out of his hair and emerged, loaded for bear, ready to indulge in his specialty—the practice of medicine as a performing art.

Over the next nine hours, Dr. Sunshine examined twenty-four

patients in minute detail, wrote fifty-one prescriptions with his favorite pen (labeled "Hufstead's Mortuary"), and returned thirty-seven phone calls with the charm of a radio talk-show host. (On a scratch pad, he doodled remarkable likenesses of the patients at the other end of the line.)

He wrapped the punishing office hours of his solo practice around a forty-five-minute lunch break with his friend-the-psychiatrist, Dr. Samuel Horowitz. (Since giving up his pursuit of women, Dr. Sunshine was allowing himself less time for lunch and more time for patients.)

Dr. Sunshine flew through each working day haunted by the fear that if he slowed down, he would never get out of the office at night. Even at full tilt, he was alert to the subtlest clinical detail—from a slightly depressed red blood cell count to a hint of yellow in an eyeball.

After thirteen years of riding herd on his huge, clamorous practice, he had recently lost some of his zip. The gravitational pull of his urge to take a nap at three o'clock each afternoon was almost more than two cups of black coffee could resist. By March of 1978, Dr. Hillel Sunshine had, as he put it, been downgraded from a hurricane to a tropical storm.

Like any freak of nature, Hurricane Hilly had been unpredictable. To trace its origin and its path of destruction, one must ignore the charts of the meteorologist and consult those of the astrologist.

THE ZODIAC TOUR '76–'77

6 SUNDAY, MARCH 21, 1976

ARIES WITH VIRGO

Gift in hand, he barged through the garden gate of the redhead's cottage on Allston Way. He was grateful she had warned him about the antitank gun. Mounted on her front lawn, it was pointed directly at him. She had started to tell him on the phone that her stepfather, a GI during World War II, had "liberated" the Polish gun from a Nazi weapons depot. But Dr. Sunshine was more interested in nailing down directions to her house and confirming the time she expected him. She had always asked only one thing of him— to be on time.

At the stroke of eight, he rang her front door bell. From within, her rich, commanding voice cried, "Close your eyes!" A moment later, she threw open the door and flung herself into his arms. With his eyes dutifully shut, her tall visitor mumbled an apology for being a half hour late and slowly became aware, through his keen sense of touch, that his petite, shapely hostess was dressed only in bra and panties.

"Yoo-hoo, I'm down here," she said, impulsively grabbing his proffered box of perfume with one hand and his crotch with the other. Dr. Sunshine, for once, was at a loss for words.

"Oh," she said, "how sweet—Charlie."

"Actually, I call him Poindexter," he said, blushing scarlet.

"Doctor, I was referring to the perfume."

"Oh. Sorry."

"Don't apologize—but never keep me waiting again," she said, giving Poindexter a playful squeeze that almost ruined everything.

Expectantly flushed and quickly naked, the beauteous Aries propped herself up on three down pillows in her carefully unmade bed. With mounting irritation, she watched the handsome Virgo methodically remove and fastidiously arrange his jacket, vest, shirt, tie, shoes, pants, socks, shirt, Jockey shorts, and glasses.

At length, he slipped into bed and whispered, "Valerie—wake up."

Ten minutes later, during a climactic moment, his beeper, of all things, went off.

"What was that?" she moaned.

"My beeper."

"Where is it?"

"Over there, on top of my Jockeys."

"Godammit! Who could possibly want to disturb you now, of all times?"

"It's probably God. He's left a message with my answering service that I should be ashamed of myself."

"Well, tell your answering service to reroute God's call to Dial-a-Prayer, and come right back to bed."

While the sun was in Aries from March 21 through April 20, 1976, Sunshine was in the house of Valerie Lustbender twice a day. In honor of their affair, she hung a large, framed print of "The Kiss" by Klimt over the head of her bed. Dr. Sunshine agreed that he and Ms. Lustbender bore an uncanny resemblance to the dark-haired man and the redheaded woman in the picture. In Gustav Klimt, Dr. Sunshine recognized a man who adored redheads almost as much as he did.

Too soon for both of them, the Aries and her Virgo reached the far cusp of their relationship. On their last night, as they lay entwined in each other's limbs, she murmured into his ear, "When you call me on the phone, it's like the sound of rain after a heat wave. When you walk through the front door, it's like Olivier stepping through the curtains at Drury Lane. When you first go inside me, it's like the sun coming up."

Inspired by her eloquence, he looked deeply into her shining green eyes and said, "Really?"

She snuggled closer. Soon, his resolve to ditch Aries and move on to Taurus began to shrivel, as Poindexter stiffened. With considerable effort, he intoned some mumbo jumbo about having to get back to his family and mend some fences. To his delight, she bought it. Or seemed to—with just a few tears and a tremulous smile.

"I hate to break it off so soon," he said, backing out her front door. "You've been wonderful, Val—please keep in touch."

The next morning, she called his office and proposed a suicide pact. ("You first, you bastard!") As her tirade escalated, he interrupted to give her the name of Dr. Samuel Horowitz, a psychiatrist. He assured her that Dr. Horowitz would be willing to meet with her that afternoon and help her cope with her "separation anxiety." Dr. Sunshine said that he would foot the bill—and that he had made a mistake and was terribly sorry. The sound of her receiver banging down blunted the hearing in his right ear for two weeks.

7   FRIDAY, MARCH 24, 1978
      6:17 P.M. BERKELEY

The redheaded antitank gunner studied the digital watch on her left wrist: . . . *28 . . . 29 . . . 30 . . .*

Crump

It was not so much a noise as a faint impact. The fire bomb in the warehouse at 10th and Stuart Streets had gone off precisely on schedule. The gunner smiled and looked up to see a plume of black smoke rising in the southwest above twilit Berkeley. Thirty seconds later, a duet of sirens—first the contralto fire engine, then the soprano squad car—sang of the success of the diversionary tactic.

The gunner looked down darkening Oxford Street—no Mercedes in sight. Of all the Virgos she had known, Dr. Sunshine was the least punctual. Late, as she had predicted, for his own funeral. Her sudden fury inflamed her cheeks no less crimson than had her former lust for him.

"At least," she consoled herself, "this is the last time I have to wait for Dr. Sunshine."

Meanwhile, Earth, that working Mother, having earned a coin for her day's labor, held open a purse of gray fog to receive the gold piece of the setting sun.

Ignoring this cosmic payoff, the redhead looked again down the street.

"Oh Jesus, a Mercedes . . . "

8 FRIDAY, MARCH 24, 1978 12:34 P.M. BERKELEY

In the center of the crowded Yen Ching Restaurant on College Avenue, the two physicians hugged one another. Dr. Sunshine's woolen vest pressed against Dr. Horowitz's yucca-fibered shirt in an obligatory, nonsexual, manly Berkeley embrace—initiated, without enthusiasm, by Horowitz, detested, without reservation, by Sunshine.

"Sorry I'm late, Sam," said the internist.

"So what else is new?" said the psychiatrist. "You were always late for your appointments with me. Sit."

The two doctors crawled into opposite sides of a booth.

"Sam, I'm starving," said Dr. Sunshine, inhaling the pungent garlic-and-onion aroma of the restaurant. "Let's get a menu."

"Relax, Hilly. I've already ordered."

"What're we having?"

"Hot and sour soup, chicken with black-bean sauce, and mushu pork."

"Terrific," said Dr. Sunshine. "That sounds a lot healthier than the Valium and Dexamyl you *used* to order for me."

"Those were for your midlife crisis. This is for your middle-aged spread."

"God, I'm hungry!" said Dr. Sunshine. "Sam, ask the waiter if they serve the rhinoceros on Friday."

"Oh, Victor," signaled Dr. Horowitz to an elderly Chinese man in a red jacket. "Is it too late to add a half-order of the albino rhino, Peking style? You know, with the hide served on the side?"

The waiter stared through the psychiatrist.

"Sam, don't let him forget the horn," said Dr. Sunshine. "It's supposed to be a potent aphrodisiac."

"I'm horny enough already," said Dr. Horowitz, "but if you insist, I'll have him put it in a doggy bag for you. Confucius say, 'Impotence, like charity, begins at home.'"

"That's hitting below the belt, Sam," said Dr. Sunshine.

"Hilly, I was *kidding*. Don't tell me you've become impotent again? I thought we straightened that out years ago."

"We did. It's just that once in a blue moon, I'll suffer a regional power failure. I don't think that's a rare phenomenon at forty-three, do you?"

"Not at all. My summer house at Lake Tahoe was erected, so to speak, on fees collected from your fellow sufferers."

"What did you name it? 'Wee Pecker in the Pines?'"

The food arrived, all three dishes at once—the waiter's initial revenge. After their first taste of hot and sour soup, the two physicians began coughing and weeping copiously, so heavily spiced was the soup with pepper oil—the waiter's second revenge.

"Ice water!" rasped Dr. Horowitz, with what sounded like his last breath.

The waiter took his time—his third revenge—before presenting the two doctors with a pair of scratched glasses of warm water—his final revenge—the Chinese water torture.

"Tell the truth, Hilly," said Dr. Horowitz, when they were into the somewhat milder chicken with black-bean sauce, "if you had to choose, which would you give up—food or sex?"

Dr. Sunshine paused. "French or Chinese?" he asked.

"You're stalling, Hilly. French or Chinese what—the food or the sex?"

"Sam, let me put it this way—I'd rather be all steamed up over a Chinese dumpling than embroiled with a French lamb chop. On the other hand, I'd give up a little fortune cookie for a French tart any day in the week."

"Just like an internist—you've confused the issue hopelessly."

"Sam, you didn't invite me to lunch after one year just to get my views on food and sex. They should be quite familiar to you after what we went through during my therapy."

"You're right, Hilly. I really just wanted to touch base with you. I don't see why our relationship should end simply because we terminated your therapy. And I can't help but observe that you haven't sent me a referral in more than a year."

Dr. Sunshine blushed. "Oh, Sam. I can never repay you for what you did for me—and my wife, and all the patients I referred to you. I guess you're part of a past I've chosen to bury. Can you understand that?"

"More than you think."

The waiter plunked down two fortune cookies and a check. The right hands of the two doctors pounced simultaneously on the check, shattering the cookies.

"Sorry, Hilly. I'll take care of it. You just got through saying you can never repay me."

"Thanks, Sam. What does your fortune say?"

Through gold-rimmed glasses, Dr. Horowitz's brown eyes squinted at a thin slip of paper. " 'Sweet revenge sours quickly,' " he recited. "How about yours?"

"Mine says, 'Few can afford the price of free love.' "

THE ZODIAC TOUR '76–'77

9 WEDNESDAY, APRIL 21, 1976
TAURUS WITH VIRGO

His pale blonde Taurus in the Karl Marx T-shirt was the first avowed Communist he had ever slept with. Among other things, he was fascinated by the way her breasts made the eyes of Karl Marx bulge. Except for her tendency while making love to utter "Mao" instead of a moan, he found that her political affiliation did not make her an especially strange bedfellow.

She lived on the bottom floor of a redwood-shingled duplex in the flowered flatlands near the campus. (The social stratification of Berkeley roughly followed local topography. Those in the upper economic and academic strata lived in the hills; the proletariat, in the lowlands.) Not above mingling with the masses, Dr. Sunshine drove down from the hills at 8:00 P.M. in response to a prearranged "emergency house call" on Hillegass Avenue.

After Dr. Sunshine rapped on the brass knocker, he and Poindexter stood before the front door, ready, as the expression goes, to pole-vault into the living room. From within, the sudden loud, deep barking of what he judged to be a starving timber wolf cooled his ardor by several degrees (and Poindexter's by as many inches). He was a cat man, himself. Berkeley's running dogs of Marxism, as he called them, were a constant source of anguish to him. From their foul breath to their voluminous turds, he found them, without exception, to be shaggy abominations.

"Stay, Chuko, stay!" shouted a female voice through the canine din behind the front door.

A racket of chains and thrown bolts ensued and there they stood—mistress and dog, distaff and mastiff. Her pale, slim hand grabbed the short hair behind his loathsome neck. An overfed Siberian husky, Chuko came up to her navel and seemingly went on for yards.

"Quiet, Chuko! Stay! It's okay, Chuko. This is Dr. Sunshine. Chuko—stay."

"Chuko stay, Dr. Sunshine go," said the visitor, turning on his heel.

"Wait a minute, Hilly," she said. "I'll lock him in the kitchen."

"Take your time," said Dr. Sunshine.

After five noisy minutes, she reappeared at the door, her normally pale face exuding a Commie pink glow from her labor in the kitchen.

"You can come in now," she said.

He could have sworn that the face of Karl Marx on her tee shirt actually winked at him.

"Are you sure that Chuko can't get out?"

"Positive. I've got him chained to the kitchen table."

"And he doesn't buy the party line that he has nothing to lose but his chains?"

"No," she said, beginning to pout.

Reluctantly, Dr. Sunshine stepped over the threshold.

"As you may have gathered," he said, "I'm not a dog fancier."

"Most chickens aren't," she said, flashing a most disarming smile. "Don't worry. The next time you drop by, I'll have him eating out of your hand."

"Eating what out of my hand? My knuckles?"

She laughed and pulled off her tee shirt, making the eyes of Dr. Sunshine bulge. She hugged him and said, "I'm going to slip into something more comfortable—my bed. Join me?"

Soon, she was crying "Mao!" and he was shouting "Rockefeller!" Their ideological exchange was interrupted by a racket from the kitchen.

"What was that?" asked Dr. Sunshine.

"Nothing, just Chuko straining at his leash . . . Oh, Hilly, whatever you're doing, don't stop . . . Mao!"

For quite some time, the doctor did not stop, could not stop. He was so pre-occupied, in fact, that he did not hear the scraping of the dismembered table leg across the hardwood floor of the bedroom. Although his hearing was momentarily impaired, his sensitivity to touch and pain were keenly intact. The sudden pressure of the husky's cold, wet nose against his left buttock produced a curious, but not unpleasant sensation. What gave him pause was the bite that followed.

His grand-operatic scream frightened the dog out of the room and caused his partner to exclaim, "Oh, Hilly, are you coming already?"

"No, darling, I'm going already. Chuko just bit me in the ass."

They scrambled out of bed. When she turned on the bedroom light, they each examined the wound, he with the aid of a hand mirror.

"It looks like he broke the skin, but didn't draw any blood," she said, gently squeezing the wound. "Oops, yes he did."

"Ship him back to Siberia."

"I'm so sorry, Hilly," she said, almost succeeding in keeping a straight face. "You better take a shower. I'll look for a Band-Aid."

After reassuring him that Chuko had had his rabies shots, she joined him in the shower. With soapy hands, she gently cleansed his wound. So salubrious were her ministrations, that the two of them were able to complete in the shower what Chuko had so rudely interrupted in bed.

Thereafter, she took pains to lock up Chuko securely whenever the doctor paid a call. She double-chained the dog to the U-shaped steel pipe under the kitchen sink.

"Even if he tears loose the sink," she reassured him, "he'd never get it through the door."

On their last night together, after he announced that he could no longer see her, she excused herself for a moment and unleashed Chuko to run with him to his car. Before driving away, he was more than happy to leave the right sleeve of his suit jacket between Chuko's teeth as a farewell gift.

10 FRIDAY, MARCH 24, 1978
6:25 P.M. BERKELEY

In a phone booth outside the Texaco station on Oxford Street, a tall, slender blonde in Levi's and a red Karl Marx tee shirt looked up in rapture at the East Bay hills looming more than one thousand feet above the campus. She watched the full circumference of the remarkably large moon clear the upper branches of a eucalyptus grove.

"Oh lover, what a night to die," she thought.

She peered down Oxford—no Mercedes in sight. She teased open the Burger King bag in her right hand and felt for the heft of the Taurus .357 inside. Her fingertips grazed its muzzle, touched its trigger. She imagined firing it at her expensively tailored victim seated behind the wheel of his luxury sedan.

"One less fucking capitalist," she thought.

✳ ✳ ✳

In the ladies' room of the Texaco station on Oxford Street near Center, a well-turned, fair-skinned brunette dressed in Levi's and a yellow tank top shoved a pair of twelve-gauge shells into the chambers of a Browning B 2000. After taking aim at the tampon dispenser, the comely Gemini replaced the sawed-off shotgun inside its violin case. She took a final drag on her joint and stepped outside. She felt giddy, elated—as would any heavenly Twin about to empty double barrels into a two-timer.

✪ ✪ ✪

With feline stealth a lean, black woman dropped to her hands and knees behind a juniper bush five yards downhill and to the left of the antitank gun. Moonlight caught the stone-sharpened edge of the jewel-handled dagger in her hand. The whites of her murderous eyes glowed phosphorescently as she glanced south down Oxford. Tonight, she thought, this Leo would find out what every pussycat longs to know: was he a man or a mouse?

✪ ✪ ✪

The slim-hipped Virgo rested the walnut stock of her M-30 Drilling rifle on the sidewalk. She was hidden from passing cars by a coffin-sized signal box opposite the crosswalk at University and Oxford. The mouths of the German rifle's three barrels were pressed into her pelvis. She was not concerned; she had made sure the Greener-type safety was locked.

If her luck held, she would perforate her victim three ways: with a 3.5-mm shot cartridge from the right barrel, a Brenneke slug from the left barrel, and a 9-mm cartridge from the under-rifle barrel. She recalled how her victim used to order Tanqueray gin: a triple shot, neat, with a twist. Minus the twist, she was about to deliver just what the doctor ordered.

✪ ✪ ✪

Built on the lines of a nineteenth-century public library, the imposing, bookish Libra sat on a bench at the Oxford and Center bus stop. She absently thumbed the pages of a paperback edition of *Finnegans Wake*. There was a frown on her dimpled face and a bayonet-mounted M-1 Garand rifle in her lap. The gun was wrapped in a granny afghan.

The Libran had not yet decided whether to shoot her victim or bayonet him. She would agonize up to the last moment about which weapon to use and, in the end, use both.

☼ ☼ ☼

Not a trace of Libran ambiguity troubled the rapt face of the lithe woman jogging up Oxford. She wore purple running pants and a white tank top, each a size too small for her. Her silver Scorpio pendant danced over her large, bobbing breasts. At the sight of her, seasoned woman-watchers of both sexes stopped in their tracks. She was late, damn it, and the 20-cc plastic syringe in her right hand was leaking badly. She had better hurry, she thought, or her former Sugar Daddy would miss his evening dose of insulin.

☼ ☼ ☼

When the curvaceous, auburn-haired English Sagittarian bent down to pick up the steel-tipped arrow she had dropped on the sidewalk, a young seminary student walking behind her faltered momentarily, gaped, then made a decision that would change his life. Within a month, he would forsake the cloth for a bartender's towel. The woman responsible for this triumph of "bottoms up" over "mea culpa" almost dropped the arrow again. Compared to her own tautness, the high-strung bow on her back was slack indeed.

☼ ☼ ☼

The tiniest frown creased the lightly powdered skin of the petite Capricorn's forehead. When the Walk sign flashed, she ran with mincing steps in her metal-tipped boots to the opposite corner. The red sparks flying when her heels struck the pavement suggested that of the twelve members of the group, she was not, by far, the least to be reckoned with.

☼ ☼ ☼

From the top of her Giants' baseball cap to the tip of her gold-ringed toes, the fortyish, blue-eyed beauty was every inch an Aquarian. A one-carat diamond sparkled in the right side of her nose. To represent

Neptune's trident, she toted a three-pronged pitchfork over her right shoulder. She inflicted a beatific smile on everyone who stared at her. "Outta my way, motherfuckers," she thought. Pedestrians gave wide berth to this hell-bent child of Saturn as she twinkle-toed up University toward Oxford. Clearly, here was one Water Bearer who had wearied of carrying a torch.

❂ ❂ ❂

Bringing up the rear of this unholy procession was a Piscean whose own rear, truth to tell, needed no bringing up. Every now and then, Mother Nature tires of copying art and reproduces, instead, the centerfold of a magazine. The extravagantly shaped young woman brandishing the underwater speargun was, to quote her former physician, "a water-clear blonde." Her porcelain complexion gleamed in the purpling twilight. She marched just ahead of an impatient darkness, toward the last rays of sunshine.

11 FRIDAY, MARCH 24, 1978 6:03 P.M. BERKELEY

Mrs. Hattie Jackson, age sixty-seven, hypertensive, black and jolly, had been his patient for thirteen years. Both were smiling as Dr. Sunshine wrapped a blood pressure cuff around her left upper arm. The manometer read 140 over 80, lower than the previous month's figures.

"The blood pressure's looking good tonight," said the doctor.

"Must be that new pill you put me on," said the patient. "Thanks for all the free samples."

"You're welcome, Hattie."

"I know those little devils cost a buck apiece at the drugstore."

"I've got some more saved up for you when these run out."

"Thank you, Dr. Sunshine. Say, how come you still charge me only twelve dollars a visit? You ain't raised your prices on me in thirteen years!"

"Maybe it's because I love you, Hattie," said Dr. Sunshine, dispensing another full smile.

Mrs. Jackson suddenly became solemn as he pressed the bell of his stethoscope over her expansive left breast and listened to her heart. For a few moments, the tired doctor leaned dreamily into the soft bulwark of Hattie Jackson's torso and let the quiet *lub-dup* of her heartbeat soothe him. (Unlike his many self-professed liberal colleagues in Berkeley, such as Maury Plotkin, Dr. Sunshine was the only one who saw a substantial number of black patients.) At last, he straightened up and rechecked her blood pressure. It was now only 130 over 70.

"Hattie, you're doing fine," he said. "I'd like to see you again in two months. Call Mrs. Katz tomorrow for an appointment."

"Thank you, Dr. Sunshine. You know somethin'? You're the best doc in the whole world! I tell all my friends how lucky I am . . . "

12 FRIDAY, MARCH 24, 1978
6:10 P.M. BERKELEY

Dr. Sunshine loved the rush of silence into his office after the last patient had left. A yawn momentarily straightened his large, aquiline nose. He pulled off his horn-rimmed glasses and gave his eyeballs a knuckle massage. Then he flung his arms above his head in a bone-cracking stretch. Meditation time.

He flicked off the light in his consultation room and sat down in his leather swivel chair. He waited for his first easy breath. Then he began reciting to himself his two-hundred-dollar mantra, "Shareem," each time he exhaled. He felt his taut body relax, his overloaded brain lighten. At 6:17 P.M., just six minutes after his gentle slide into oblivion, he was jerked awake by the sound of a faint, insistent rapping on the front door of his office.

Cautiously he opened the door to his waiting room and found standing before him a startling vision from his past—a slender, beautiful woman of a certain age, in a low-cut, red silk dress. A radiant smile dimpled her lovely face.

Dr. Sunshine did a double take.

"Louise? Is that you?"

"Good diagnosis, Doctor."

After motioning her into his office, he closed the door and said, "I almost didn't recognize you. You look, uh—different."

"You mean younger."

"Well, yes," he said, studying her girlishly flirtatious brown eyes. "You're more beautiful than I've ever seen you. And it's been years! Those great genes of yours!"

"That great plastic surgeon of mine, is more like it. What you're seeing, Hilly, is more cosmetic than genetic. He took ten years off my face and added four inches to my bust."

When they had seated themselves on two comfortable lounge chairs in his spacious rear examining room, he asked, "Louise, what can I do for you?"

"First, let me apologize for dropping by unannounced. I would have called first, but I was afraid you'd tell me to get lost."

"Never."

Dr. Sunshine's hands suddenly turned clammy, and Poindexter began feeling deep nostalgic stirrings.

"Hilly, last year I married again." She raised her perfectly manicured left hand and flashed a four-carat diamond ring that made him blink despite his tinted glasses.

"How wonderful!" he said, surprised at feeling a twinge of jealousy.

"You permanently cured me of my widowhood by reigniting me seven years ago. I've been having the time of my life ever since."

"Who's the lucky guy?"

"Actually, you are. I've come to settle an erotic debt."

She stood up and took a step toward Dr. Sunshine, who jumped to his feet. Flashing a smile more brilliant than her ring, she held out her hands to him. Dr. Sunshine lightly grasped them.

"You don't owe me anything," he said.

"I was the first woman you made love to outside your marriage. I've always felt guilty about that. I want you to be the first man I make love to outside mine. I've never stop loving you, Hilly. Isn't that ridiculous? I've married a wonderful guy, but when he and I are close I always fantasize about you. Please, darling. Just this once. I won't bother you again." She gently pulled his hands down to her slim waist.

"Louise, I've never been so happy to see you. But believe it or not, I'm monogamous again. I've become one of those dreaded 'monogs' we used to make fun of. Louise, I'm not straying anymore."

Even as he protested, the fingers of his right hand began lowering the zipper of her tight-fitting dress. The dichotomy between his actions and his words was due to a neurologic reflex arc traveling from Poindexter to his spinal cord and out to his hand, completely bypassing his brain.

"Well, I suppose I shouldn't tempt you any further," she said, caressing the rapidly enlarging bulge Poindexter was making to the right of the doctor's zipper.

"I've been through hell getting back to Gloria," he said, undoing her belt buckle. "And nothing can persuade me to play around again." He pulled off his jacket. "We can't *do* this here," he concluded.

Ten minutes later, they were both flushed with the afterglow of spent lust as they sorted out their scattered clothes, and dressed quickly.

"Hilly, that was marvelous! You're more magnificent than ever . . . Darling, I'm sure you're in a hurry to get home. And so am I!"

"Oh, Louise, you've done it again," he said, embracing her. "You've hooked me. You're fantastic!"

"So are you. Good night, my love."

"Good night, Louise."

"Shall I keep in touch?"

"Please do," said Dr. Sunshine, closing the door.

In an effort to quiet his racing heart and ease his self-loathing, he tried to resume meditating. It was no go. Poindexter, for one, refused to cooperate, pointedly ignoring his mantra.

He had done it again! With Louise! Couldn't say no!

"Oh Gloria, forgive me!" he cried out. "Never again!" he vowed once again.

Before going out the door, he quickly checked his In box. He flipped through half a dozen lab slips—a few abnormal values, nothing fatal. He deep-sixed an engraved invitation to attend a seminar on "Sex after Forty" for physicians and their wives at Squaw Valley in June. (Why should he schlep his wife to a conference at six thousand feet on middle-aged sex when they had all they could handle at a thousand? ("Oh, Glory Baby, what have I done!") He also tossed in the wastebasket all fourteen of the day's influx of unsolicited magazines published by drug companies. He read a few painfully inked lines from eighty-year-old Mabel Duncan, the president of his fan club, informing him that she had put up thirty jars of jam and would appreciate a house call from him some morning when he wasn't too busy.

He tore to shreds a letter from an "Investment Counselor" who promised tax-sheltered nirvana in oil lease backs and pistachio trees. He shuddered recalling the eighty thousand dollars he had lost in ten-thousand-dollar chunks as a "Limited Partner" in various disasters. (The most recent was the Fox Tower Apartments in Los Angeles, whose last report had boasted, "The frequency of rape and armed robbery in our main elevator has dropped substantially since the first quarter.")

He also threw out requests for donations to save whales, elect congressmen, and support Planned Parenthood. He got up to leave, half-expecting the small garage under his building to be filled with dead whales, defeated politicians, pregnant teenyboppers—and his wife.

THE ZODIAC TOUR '76–'77

13 SATURDAY, MAY 22, 1976
GEMINI WITH VIRGO

All his adult life he had been the willing victim of the awesome power of beautiful women.

"You are forever staring at women like a charmed snake," his wife had observed shortly after their marriage.

As usual, his wife was bang-on, but she could not have guessed how charmed he was, nor how much of a snake. His willingness to be tied down by his Gemini was a case in point.

Like most women of great beauty, his Gemini was highly intelligent. Her facile success in a so-called man's world embarrassed her. In her second *year as a sales rep for a computer software company, she netted over $150K. Dr. Sunshine was the first man she had met who did not quake before the dazzle of her appearance and the size of her income.*

In fact, until he came into her life, she had been a social recluse. Out of boredom, she studied belly dancing three nights a week. The other nights she stayed home reading straight through the fifteenth edition of the Encyclopedia Britannica. *She had reached page 723,* METAMORPHIC–NEW JERSEY, *when Dr. Sunshine diagnosed her mitral valve prolapse and captured her heart in the process.*

The fair-skinned, blue-eyed brunette in a belly-dancer outfit knelt in the center of her bed. "I've always wanted to do this." she said. "Now just lie still, Hilly. Believe me, for my dancing, I need a captive audience."

With twisted lengths of panty hose, she was tying the doctor's wrists and ankles to the four posts of her brass bed.

"When I undressed and climbed into bed," said Dr. Sunshine, "this was not what I had in mind."

"Turnabout is fair play, Doctor," she said. "When I was lying down in your office, you strapped all my *limbs in light bondage."*

"But that was to take your EKG.*"*

"Yes, and my aching heart with its floppy valve went pitter-pat, remember? So will yours, when I'm through with you . . . There."

Having secured her doctor, the bangled, heavily made-up Gemini jingled out of bed and turned up to full volume a record of belly-dance music on her hi-fi. After lighting a scented candle, she turned off the overhead light and began dancing in a frenzy about the bed. The doctor toyed with the notion of interrupting her to ask if he could make tinkle in the bathroom, but there was so much noise and so little light, he could not think of an effective way to capture her attention.

As a belly dancer, he observed, she was no great shakes. But what she lacked in talent, she made up for in kinetic energy. During one of her whirling turns about the bed, she slipped on a throw rug and slammed head-first into the side of a bookcase. She dropped like a frozen rope to the floor, and lay perfectly still.

"Oh boy," said the doctor. His eyes changed from those of a charmed snake to those of a trapped rat.

With his peripheral vision, he ascertained that she was still breathing. In the next hour and a half, the worst thing he suffered was the music. The deafening whine of nasal instruments and the cacophony of ill-struck bells slowly increased to a vertiginous tempo and then abruptly stopped, only to start up again on the automatic turntable.

The third time the music stopped, she raised her head from the floor and said, "Dr. Sunshine—what are you doing here? Oh, my God—my head! Doctor, help me."

"I can't. I'm tied up at the moment."

"How did that happen?"

"Take it easy. You're probably suffering temporary amnesia. Please untie me."

Moving more slowly than any belly dancer in history, she released him from his nylon bondage. After a quick trip to the bathroom, Dr. Sunshine confined the stricken patient to bed, where they spent the next half hour comforting one another.

"There-there," said the good doctor, gently guiding her hand towards Poindexter.

"Here-here?" she asked.

"Yes, there-there."

14 FRIDAY, MARCH 24, 1978
6:32 P.M. BERKELEY

The sight of his Mercedes still embarrassed him. It had been only six weeks since his closest friend and most devoted patient, Dr. Ernesto Gianini, had bequeathed him the light-green 450 SEL. Gianini's widow, Minerva, had insisted that Sunshine keep the Mercedes.

"Ernie loved you, Hilly, and that's the truth," she said. "Take it. You were wonderful to Ernie. Look, I've still got my XKE."

Dr. Ernesto Gianini, a retired general practitioner, had been Dr. Sunshine's friend for ten years, since the day the older man panted into the internist's office, bearing copies of Boswell's *Johnson* and Schirer's *The Rise and Fall of the Third Reich*. Since Dr. Sunshine didn't charge Dr. Gianini for treating the latter's hopelessly atherosclerotic heart, the two of them ate at the fabled Jack's Restaurant in San Francisco every Wednesday for a decade, at Gianini's expense.

The young internist found in his aging and failing friend a fount of sparkling conversation on every subject under the sun, with the notable and desired exception of medicine. Literature, history, opera, sex, and politics kept the two doctors shouting and laughing above the alcohol-fueled din of Jack's at lunchtime. Formerly a ravenous eater, Ernie hardly touched his food, contenting himself to enjoy, vicariously, Hilly's boundless appetite for Jack's mutton chops, creamed spinach, and deep-fried eggplant.

And now, despite every trick Hilly could pull out of his doctor's bag, Ernie was dead. And the general practitioner's gorgeous Mercedes now belonged to the internist. He only wished the damn thing wasn't German.

The one subject on which Dr. Sunshine had been more passionate than Dr. Gianini was Nazi Germany. The Holocaust, and then Israel, had made Dr. Sunshine, if not a devout Jew, then a determined one. He vowed never to set foot on German soil, never to own a German car, and never, if he could help it, to treat a non-Jewish German patient.

To anyone who asked him about his name, Dr. Sunshine took pains to point out that his family was originally from Poland. His branch of the Sobranski clan acquired the Germanic name, Sonnenschein, only as protective coloration when a maverick ancestor, Jacob, emigrated to Bavaria in 1825.

Polish anti-Semitism was only slightly less repugnant to Dr. Sunshine than German anti-Semitism. His favorite European country was Denmark, whose king had worn the yellow star as a signal to the occupying Nazis to keep their hands off his Jewish subjects. Dr. Sunshine spent his career waiting for a Danish patient, whom he could treat like a king and charge nothing.

Instead, he ended up with the largest number of non-Jewish German patients in Berkeley. Possibly in keeping with their old country's tradition (shared by Hitler's family) of seeking out the best Jewish doctor in town, they had converged on his office in Volkswagens, Audis, Porsches, BMWs, and Mercedes. And were they charming! And handsome! And artistic! And, of course, anti-Nazi!

Their eyes all—without exception—blazed.

Dr. Sunshine treated them with the skill and courtesy of a field surgeon ministering to the enemy. He even admired his German patients, but could not look them in the eye, except with an ophthalmoscope.

And then his dearest friend had played his cruelest joke on him—left him the Mercedes. Dr. Sunshine couldn't insult his widow by refusing the gift. And the Mercedes, after all, was, like his German patients, handsome, efficient, obedient. It was also worth something in the neighborhood of thirty thousand dollars and Hilly, Ernie knew, was not indifferent to the charms of luxury.

Dr. Sunshine's final rationalization for accepting the car was that it was splendid armor plating for him and his family. Compared to his Datsun 260Z and his wife's Valiant station wagon, the Mercedes was a tank. Small wonder Hitler had chosen a 7.3-liter Mercedes in which to tool around the fatherland. And now the descendent of Jacob Sonnenschein was in the driver's seat of a 4.5-liter version of the Jew-killer's chariot.

In order to make sure Dr. Sunshine fully appreciated the glee Dr. Gianini had taken in forcing the Mercedes on him, Ernesto had taken pains to tape, for the new owner's listening pleasure, a cassette of musical selections. The latter included, among others, "The Horst Wessel Song," "Deutschland Uber Alles," "Springtime for Hitler," and several hair-raising excerpts from Wagner. In his fine Italian hand, Ernesto had written the title for this pastiche on the front of the cassette: *Hum Along with Hitler*.

Dr. Sunshine felt he owed Dr. Gianini the posthumous satisfaction of playing the uncomfortably stirring pieces from time to time. It was the steep price he was willing to pay for the Mercedes.

At 6:39 P.M. on the evening of Friday, March 24, 1978, Dr. Hillel Isaiah Sunshine drove out of his office garage behind the wheel of a light-green Mercedes 450 SEL with "The Horst Wessel Song" blaring from its four Blaupunkt speakers.

THE ZODIAC TOUR '76–'77

15 WEDNESDAY, JULY 7, 1976
CANCER WITH VIRGO

The tall, thin ex-model sat across the desk from him with her alabaster face half-buried in her hands. Slowly she ran her silver fingernails through her jet-black hair. "Ten shark fins cutting through a night sea," thought Dr. Sunshine, doodling on a scratch pad. She looked up at him with her enormous, dark-circled, brown eyes. Her bloodless lips—which, when painted a dark, sticky red for TV commercials, had sold millions of tubes of lipstick— barely moved as she asked, "Why am I exhausted all the time?"

After his Moonchild's first visit to his office, he had correctly diagnosed her as having unipolar depression. Three weeks after taking the mood elevator he had prescribed, she emerged briefly, but dramatically, from her despair. With her arms wide open, she stood in the middle of his consultation room and said, "For the first time in five years, I think I want a man to kiss me." He made a tentative step forward and the Crab suddenly had him in her pincers, the bivalve of her famous lips parting as he bent to kiss her. . . .

Her gloomy cottage rested in the perpetual shade of a eucalyptus grove off one of the serpentine roads wriggling up the Berkeley hills. The melancholic Moonchild was continuing to respond nicely to her antidepressant pill. Now, instead of awaking at 3:00 A.M. and pacing the floor till dawn, she awoke at 4:00, phoned Suicide Prevention, chatted with the volunteer for a few minutes, then quickly cried herself back to sleep.

She always insisted that Dr. Sunshine split a bottle of wine with her before they retired to her waterbed. She also introduced the doctor to marijuana, which, when combined with the wine, had the effect she desired of prolonging his efforts to arouse her.

Until she met Dr. Sunshine, no man had ever succeeded in bringing her to orgasm.

Oh, how Poindexter rose to this challenge! Oh, how the doctor bent to his task! The first night with her, he developed both tennis elbow and lockjaw

from his herculean efforts at foreplay. Their exertions on the waterbed in-
duced waves of almost tsunami proportions. After forty-five minutes of oohs,
aahs, gasps, and yes-yes-yesses, she sank back with a sob and announced,
"I can't make it, dammit—I just can't. How're you doing?"

Dr. Sunshine lay on his back like a storm-tossed dinghy, the wind knocked
out of its sails. He looked down at a slightly tilted Poindexter and said, "I feel
like Two Years Before the Mast.*"*

She grasped his starboard love handle, climbed aboard his heaving torso,
and numbly rode out the remainder of the storm. Soon they were lying at an-
chor in a becalmed sea of postcoital tristesse.

Within two weeks of seeing his despondent Cancer, Dr. Sunshine lost
eight pounds and was routinely awaking at 3:00 A.M. Along with the wine
and marijuana, he found it necessary to take Dramamine a half hour before
lying on her waterbed. His nightly voyage in search of the female orgasm
began to take on the characteristics of some of the drearier episodes of
"Jacques Cousteau."

Dr. Sunshine owed a good measure of his eventual success to her former
lover, a married Oakland firefighter who had been moonlighting with her
for six months until Sunshine eclipsed him. For years the fireman had served
as chief detonator at the annual Fourth of July fireworks display at the Oak-
land Coliseum. At the conclusion of the '76 blast, he discovered that his
brigade had failed to ignite a spectacular device that had taken an entire
Taiwanese family one year to fabricate. The huge, pear-shaped bomb, de-
signed to explode seven hundred feet in the air and give off five color bursts,
each a hundred yards long, had lain hidden under a fireproof tarp during
the show.

After dismissing his buddies, the fireman hustled the unfired Asian mas-
terpiece into his station wagon and drove home. A latent pyromaniac, he
kept the aerial bomb concealed in his garage as a possible means of off-duty
diversion when there wasn't much on TV.

When the fireman discovered that his former flame was entertaining a
new lover who wore three-piece suits, he reached for the bomb.

On the fifteenth night of his affair with the sad-eyed Cancer, Dr. Sunshine
decided to try a new tack—light touch. No more pinching, poking, prodding,
kneading. Instead, gentle palpation.

Accordingly, after pushing off into the waterbed that night, he faintly
brushed his lips against her cheek, her forehead, and her eyelids. With tremulous

fingertips, he grazed the fiberglasslike smoothness of her breasts, abdomen and hips, seeking inexorably, but with infinite patience, the steamy recess between her slender thighs.

After more than an hour of light touch and heavy breathing, he was about to abandon this technique in favor of giving her a pinch on the tush, when she suddenly moaned, "Oh Hilly . . . I think . . . I'm . . . "

At this point in time, a thirty-seven-pound bomb, remote-controlled by a fireman up in a tree, went off inside her closet. The initial explosion blew out the closet door and all four windows in the bedroom, and, incidentally, triggered the Moonchild's first orgasm.

The initial color burst was red—great, blinding, phosphorescent balls shot through the windows. The second burst was green and opened up a massive rent in the waterbed, ultimately saving the lives of the terrified occupants. The two lovers in the leaking bed were holding onto each other for dear life when the gold balls started coming. Then a great fizzing noise, plus a dense cloud of not-unpleasant-smelling smoke, filled the room. Then silence.

"God, what have I been missing all these years!" she cried. "Darling, hand me my cigarettes."

"Sweetheart," said Dr. Sunshine, wading to the bathroom, "don't you think lighting a cigarette at this time would be anticlimactic?"

16 FRIDAY, MARCH 24, 1978 6:34 P.M. BERKELEY

Dr. Sunshine was involuntarily humming "The Horst Wessel Song," as he turned right on Telegraph Avenue. He *felt* like a Nazi after what he and Louise had just done in the office. The Berkeley sky was suffused with the lavender afterglow of sunset. A full moon was rising in the east above the hills. A promise of spring rain was in the air, pervading the atmosphere with salubrious negative ions, lending the air a softness achingly reminiscent of his childhood days in Pittsburgh—Springtime for Hillel. By the time the Mercedes had made its way to Telegraph and Bancroft Way through the waning rush-hour traffic, the tape had reached the overture to *Die Walküre*.

Under Furtwängler's baton, the '37 Berlin Philharmonic, with its largely Jewish string section, painfully evoked the aura of imminent death, the appearance of the blonde Valkyries on the battlefield to select which heroes were to die, the carrying off to Valhalla of the slain warriors. In 1937, thought Sunshine, those Jewish fiddlers could not have known that Auschwitz would be their Valhalla. *Die Walküre*—more pagan German bullshit!

Dr. Sunshine turned left on Bancroft Way, the southern boundary of the U.C. Berkeley campus. On this soft spring evening, it did not escape his attention that a large number of coeds were flooding the sidewalks around the campus. For a committed woman-watcher like Sunshine, living in Berkeley was heaven. Each year thousands of gently matriculating coeds moved in to replace the graduating seniors who, by then, had lost their bloom, grown faint moustaches from birth control pills, and taken to walking like men. Ah, the freshmen girls in their lovely, unfaded jeans! Perhaps not as awesome as Irwin Shaw's young women in their summer dresses, but this was a different season in the affairs of men.

17 FRIDAY, MARCH 24, 1978 6:10 P.M. BERKELEY

From her position on the grassy knoll, the redheaded antitank gunner was the first to catch sight of the light-green Mercedes. In the last fifteen minutes, she had started, almost fatally, at the sight of several 450 SELs that had turned out to be the wrong car. At last, this was the one she had been waiting for. She checked her watch: 6:43 P.M.

"Aries to all Signs," she announced, her voice transmitted through the microphonic back of her silver pendant. "Aries to all Signs. Prepare to orbit. Prepare to orbit."

The eleven women insinuated themselves among the scores of pedestrians streaming along Oxford Street. Briskly they converged on a spot the local newspapers would mark with a large black X, resembling an Iron Cross, in the morning editions.

As viewed from the knoll, the stage was set; the leading man was about to enter, downstage left. The femmes fatales, nervously fingering their props, took their positions upstage left. As if on cue, the dusk-activated street lights first glowed dully, then poured their full pink-white phosphorescence on the street scene below.

Among the *dramatis personae* was Hillel Isaiah Sunshine, a man of many parts—Hero, Villain, Victim, Romantic Lead, Doctor in the House. Unrehearsed, he hastened from the left wing to the scene of the crime.

18 FRIDAY, MARCH 24, 1978
6:42 P.M. BERKELEY

Dr. Sunshine shot past a group of six young protesters who had lined up for an all-night vigil. Illuminated by his headlights, they stood twelve feet apart on the broad lawn before the Kennedy Memorial on the western edge of the campus. The group carried banners decrying the university's active role in nuclear weapons development. As he slowed to a stop at the corner of University and Oxford, Dr. Sunshine stared thoughtfully at the demonstrators, his social conscience piqued. He concluded that the young woman standing third from the left was not half-bad.

As he pulled away from the stop sign, a deafening explosion interrupted his erotic reverie.

After thirty-nine years of impotence, the Pozcisk suddenly discharged the full wad of its pent-up fury. The armor-piercing shell perforated the right front door of the Mercedes, ricocheted off the left front speaker and buried itself in the transmission.

En route, the screaming shell grazed the right side of the driver's chest, fracturing three of his ribs. *Die Walküre* gamely played on as Dr. Sunshine slammed on the brakes.

His first sensation was one of vast relief that the Mercedes, under his ownership, had at last suffered its first dent. His next thought centered around the terrific pain in his right side when he inhaled. He looked out his side window for assistance and was relieved to see a familiar face. Then he briefly passed out as a Taurus .357 revolver went off, creasing his skull.

Seconds later he awoke, moderately demented, staring into the open mouths of a Browning double-barreled shotgun. It was held by a woman whose turretlike breasts he was sure he had seen before, held before. Wishing an unobstructed view of her bosom, he reached out his left hand and shoved the Browning's barrel aside with some annoyance. The recoil of the blazing shotgun thrust his arm down against the window frame, cracking a small bone in his wrist. The deflected lead pellets made Swiss cheese of the glove-leather upholstery covering the back seat.

Dr. Sunshine, still punchy from his head wound, beheld another woman, another gun. He briefly swooned again, pitching forward in his shoulder harness. The Remington .44-caliber Core-Lokt bullet, aimed at his heart, passed instead behind his flexed torso, pinking off the tip of the spinous process of his fifth dorsal vertebra.

Dr. Sunshine awoke to the pleasant discovery that the pain in his rib cage had disappeared. Only his head and left wrist ached, dully.

Meanwhile, the soft Core-Lokt bullet had struck the inside of the front passenger door just above the armrest and mushroomed to produce a smoking two-foot crater in the light-green metal outside. Bemusedly Dr. Sunshine watched the mangled passenger door swing slowly open. Like a grateful hitchhiker, a beautiful black woman slipped into the seat next to him.

"Katana," he said, pleasantly surprised, "what are *you* doing here?"

Her right hand drove the dagger to its jewelled hilt into his spleen. Dr. Sunshine looked down at the pulsating haft and marvelled at not feeling any pain. She stared in wonder at his serene face.

"For the love of *Jesus*," she said, "why don't you *die*, honky?"

"Honk if I love Jesus?" he asked uncertainly. "Sweetheart, if it's all the same to you, I'll pass."

Her mission accomplished, the black Leo slid out of the car just as a white Virgin appeared at his window. She pointed a triple-barreled Drilling rifle at his head and began cursing at the top of her lungs.

"You motherfucker!" she cried. "You asshole! You piece of shit!"

Dr. Sunshine, already feeling rather put upon, understandably assumed these imprecations were being directed at him, when in reality, the young woman was railing at each of the three barrels of her silent gun.

"In what branch of the Navy did *you* serve?" he asked, waggling his right index finger at her. The Drilling's left barrel suddenly erupted. A Brenneke slug burrowed into his left shoulder.

That hurt. Puzzled that he should be feeling pain again, he grabbed his wounded shoulder with his right hand. A thirty millimeter shell from a Garand rifle passed through the open right door and blew his glasses off his nose. He was thus spared a 20/20 view of that most off-putting of sights: a bayonet charge. The tip of the bayonet nicked his right shoulder just deep enough to bring him momentarily to his senses.

"MY GOD!" he cried. "THEY'RE TRYING TO KILL ME!"

When a gorgeous brunette holding a dripping syringe appeared at his window, he called out, "Oh nurse, God bless you, is that morphine?"

"No, sweetheart—it's insulin."

She injected three hundred units of regular insulin into his left biceps. His eyes once more assumed a looney stare. "But there must be some mistake," he said. "My *mother* has diabetes, not me."

Too late, he remembered his Swiss Army knife. While he fumbled for it in his right pants pocket, an arrow zipped through the driver's window. It pierced the hand-stitched, left breast pocket of his suit and burrowed into the very heart of his leather-bound appointment book. After destroying scores of unlisted phone numbers assiduously collected over a decade, the tip of the arrow came to rest on the last page of the book, marked "Z."

Just as he succeeded in wrenching out the arrow, a petite woman with steel-tipped heels jumped down through the sunroof onto Dr. Sunshine's neck. It was the unkindest cut of all. Now he was pain-free below his neck, but he was finding it difficult to breathe and stay awake.

Dr. Sunshine slumped down in his seat and looked up into the tranquil face of a forty-three-year-old woman with a diamond in her nose. She plunged a three-pronged pitchfork into his crotch.

"Oh boy," said Dr. Sunshine.

Finally, a flawless blonde appeared at the window and administered the coup de grace: an underwater spear, shot point-blank into his chest. The insulin by this time was rapidly depressing his blood sugar concentration.

With his last breath, Dr. Sunshine blew a kiss to the blonde and plummeted into oblivion.

☉ ☉ ☉

From the grassy knoll, the redhead stood beside the smoking anti-tank gun and smiled. It had gone so well. Werner would be so proud of them. As she ran down to join her sisters in their death dance around the car, she thought to herself, "The lucky bastard—just the way he would have wanted it: surrounded by beautiful women."

19 FRIDAY, MARCH 24, 1978
6:50 P.M. BERKELEY

"And now for a look at traffic in the East Bay, we switch to Tele-copter 8 and Rod Haskins."

Viewers of Channel 8's 6:00 P.M. news saw an overhead shot of a white ribbon of headlights stretching north and a red ribbon of tail lights, south, on Highway 80 alongside the San Francisco Bay.

"As you can see, Herb," shouted the traffic reporter's voice through the sound of helicopter blades, "we've got no hang-ups on Highway 80 from the Bay Bridge Toll Plaza to Pinole . . . hey, that's funny . . . "

"What's that, Rod?" asked the anchorman in the studio.

"I don't know. Over in Berkeley I just saw a flash of fire and a tower of smoke . . . there, I think you can still see the smoke. Reminds me of 'Nam . . . "

The live camera extended to full telephoto range as the helicopter banked east toward the center of Berkeley.

"I think we're right over the problem now. Looks like a stalled ve-hicle on Oxford Street right next to the university."

The chopper dropped to one hundred feet. An overhead view of a disabled Mercedes, intensely lit by the cameraman's spotlights, filled TV screens all over the Bay Area.

"Whatever happened to that Benz, it sure looks like the driver's getting plenty of help. There must be a dozen people surrounding the vehicle. Looks like somebody's even up on the roof . . . "

Irritated that the traffic news had eaten away thirty-seven seconds of prime time instead of the allotted fifteen, the Channel 8 news director cut away from the scene of the crime to the smiling face of the anchorman.

"And now for a look at the weather . . . "

20 FRIDAY, MARCH 24, 1978
7:04 P.M. HERRICK HOSPITAL, BERKELEY

"SHEEEE-EEEEEE-IT," said Mr. Devereux, the chief orderly, shaking his gray Afro in disbelief. Like many men of few words, he was a master of inflection and nuance.

"I wouldn't shit you, man," said Mr. Clarinet, the Intensive Care nurse, who, though quite white and "très gay," was easily able to slip into the argot of the upwardly Mobile, Alabama, black.

"Not Doctah Sunshine!" said Mr. Devereux. "Who'd wanna kill *him*?"

"God knows. Probably some Telegraph Avenue creep."

The two white-uniformed men were running down the steps from Four East to the Emergency Room of Herrick Hospital. The stairwell began filling with the sound of other frantic footsteps as the intercom throughout the hospital nasally intoned, "Code Blue, Emergency Room . . . Code Blue, Emergency Room . . . "

In the E.R., it was the full production. Policemen, firemen, ambulance drivers, paramedics, nurses, winos, and wackos.

An announcement of Code Blue over a hospital intercom is a mandate for all medical personnel not otherwise engaged to come running to the designated spot. As a social mixer, a rallying cry of "Code Blue" ranks in efficacy just below "Drinks are on the house!" Physicians who haven't seen each other for years meet at Code Blues. Strange doctors whom nobody seems to recognize, come out of the woodwork. Elderly internists whom many have presumed dead for years, create sensations when they pant onto the scene. Not wishing to haul coals to Newcastle, the older boys take care not to drop dead while running to a Code Blue. The result is that the swifter youngsters get to play hero while the sluggish old-timers gather on the sidelines, kibbutz, and make nuisances of themselves.

"Looks like Laurel and Hardy got here first," observed Dr. Sidney Holstein to Dr. Milton Shapiro, a fellow silver-haired latecomer.

At the head of the dying patient, Dr. Sol "Wobbles" Weinstein, the three-hundred-pound E.R. physician, was already pumping oxygen by bag and mask. Performing closed-chest cardiac massage—reluctantly, ineptly—was Dr. Mark Abromowitz, a frail young psychiatrist who had been minding his own business when the Code Blue was called in. He had been in the E.R. trying to calm a gigantic, bellowing truck driver freaked out on Angel Dust.

Sweating profusely, Wobbles Weinstein was giving oxygen and yelling orders while visions danced in his head of an uneaten combination pizza stiffening with rigor mortis in the nurse's station.

"Who's the little one?" asked Dr. Holstein, on the sidelines.

"Don't know—a psychiatrist, by the looks of him," said Dr. Shapiro, his fellow silver fox.

"What do you know," said Dr. Holstein, "a psychiatrist. Practicing real medicine for a change. Milty, you know why you almost never see a psychiatrist out in the open?"

"No, why?"

"Because a psychiatrist is a squirrely creature who hollows out a tree trunk, drags in twelve nuts after him, and is never seen again."

Dr. Holstein and Dr. Shapiro almost went into respiratory arrest wheezing and coughing over that one.

Meanwhile, the E.R. secretary had phoned Mrs. Sunshine at home. In a broken voice, she informed her that her husband had been seriously injured in an auto accident and suggested that she come over at once. Mrs. Sunshine silently hung up the phone. With her dazed brain shifting to automatic-housewife, she walked into the kitchen, turned off the stove, and called upstairs to the children. In an excessively chirpy voice, she told them, "Mommy's got to go out for about an hour—don't worry. Make yourselves some peanut butter and jelly sandwiches and get ready for bed."

Orderly Devereux and Nurse Clarinet elbowed aside a gaggle of aging Code Blue groupies and looked down on what remained of Dr. Hillel Sunshine. Veterans of scores of Code Blues, they had never seen anything like it. Speared, stabbed, bullet-riddled, the patient resembled a one-man museum of conventional warfare. Only his uniform was wrong. The pale, bloody, middle-aged man in the expensive three-piece suit and polished black oxfords lay on his back, staring with dilated pupils into the sun-bright overhead light. His dark red, Italian silk tie perfectly matched the blood stains on his dove-gray suit. A snappy dresser, Dr. Sunshine was color coordinated to the very end.

"Dear God," said Mr. Clarinet, his eyes filling with tears.

"Shee-*it!*" said Mr. Devereux, shunting aside the frail Dr. Abromowitz. "Excuse me, Doctah," said Mr. Devereux, "but you ain't movin' no blood."

Devereux's strong brown hands replaced the psychiatrist's dainty pink ones on the center of the patient's chest. Devereux's hands depressed the patient's sternum at a precise rate of sixty times per minute. Dr. Abromowitz sighed with relief, stood up, and headed quickly in the direction of someone shouting, "I'll kill the next motherfucker who walks through that curtain!"

Nurse Clarinet felt for the patient's left femoral artery, just below one of the pitchfork wounds. (The three-pronged weapon had fallen to the street while the paramedics were hustling the patient into the ambulance.)

"You're getting a pulse, Dev," said Mr. Clarinet.

The male nurse grabbed a pair of scissors and began cutting away the sleeves of the patient's jacket.

"Get me two 18-gauge needles and two liters of Plasminate," said Clarinet to one of the female nurses gathered around the patient. "And get some pressure dressings on these wounds!"

Clarinet's hand felt the rectangular outline of the notebook through the patient's suit jacket. His hand slipped into the doctor's breast pocket. In the chaos swirling about the moribund patient, not even Devereux saw Clarinet palm the notebook and pocket it.

At the head of the patient, Wobbles Weinstein bellowed orders while he squeezed the oxygen bag.

"Hook him up to the monitor! Somebody draw blood for a stat crit and blood gases! Type and cross-match twelve units of whole blood! Get me surgeons! Vascular surgeons! Neurosurgeons! Any surgeons! Tell the O.R. we've got a hot one, turning cold."

Once again, Dr. Sunshine was surrounded by a dozen women—this time, nurses and techs—women with tears in their eyes, women who laid hands on his body therapeutically. With sharp and blunt instruments and chemical solutions—needles, catheters, drugs—they swiftly invaded his body, preparing him for the surgeon's knife. (The malpractice lawyers had been the first to appreciate the similarity of the tools of the healer to those of the killer.)

Within a minute, Mr. Clarinet had an IV bottle running wide open into both the patient's antecubital veins. Clarinet's insertion of the needles was no mean feat to perform on someone whose blood pressure was zero and whose veins had collapsed.

Police Sergeant Parnell lumbered up to the side of the patient to ask if he was dead yet.

"No!" said Clarinet, taping down the needle. "Do you guys have any idea who did this?"

"Yeah—our prime suspects right now are the Polish Army, the United Farm Workers, and Chief Crazy Horse. Our evidence already includes an antitank gun, a pitchfork, and an arrow. You sure he ain't dead yet?"

The patient's survival now hinged on elemental considerations of air and water—oxygen in his lungs and saline in his veins—needs harking back to his prehuman origins, to the gas exhaled by the forest primeval, to the salty fluid of the amniotic, Precambrian sea.

THE ZODIAC TOUR '76–'77

21 SATURDAY, JULY 24, 1976
LEO WITH VIRGO

She was the first black woman he had ever found himself in bed with. An equal-opportunity lecher, Dr. Sunshine had courted African American women before, but had always been turned down. With Katana Simms, he didn't know how to account for his good luck. She was bright, witty, charming, and had that generosity of breast and haunch that had not been in fashion since the 'fifties, the decade, according to Dr. Sunshine, that had produced the most beautiful women in American history.

At twenty-six, an assistant bank manager on her way up, she was reveling in the restrictive pleasures of middle-class America. She took no small measure of pride in paying forty dollars for an office visit to her internist for relief of a middle-management headache—a quantum leap for someone whose mother had taken Anacin for twenty-five years for housemaid's knee.

She was not quite ready for him when he knocked on the door of her posh, ninth-floor Oakland condominium. Her fingernail polish still wet, she hugged him with her wrists, then turned her smooth, supple back to him.

"Be a darling and fix my zipper."

He placed his champagne bottle on the white carpet and clumsily retracked her derailed zipper. Then he routed it straight up the back of her white, knit dressing gown.

"Thank you, Hillel," she said, flashing a blue-shadowed doe's eye over her shoulder. "Please excuse me for a moment. I'm on the phone with my boss—some last-minute jazz before he goes on vacation. Do me a favor?"

"Sure."

"Grab a package of mini-pizzas from the freezer, set the oven to three-fifty, and pop them in. Also, my damned cats got into a jar of cotton balls while I was doing my nails and are going bananas in the bathroom. See if you can distract them—there's a can of Purina Cat Chow in the kitchen cabinet above the dishwasher. The can opener's next to the Mixmaster."

"Very good, milady."

While she exchanged unpleasantries with her boss on the white Princess phone in her living room, Dr. Sunshine risked cat-scratch fever in the bathroom, rounding up her two Siamese and replacing three dozen scattered cotton balls in a glass container. He then started the hors d'oeuvres and fed the cats.

His chores completed, he walked into her immaculate bedroom. As he removed his clothes, he was struck by the fact that everything in her condo, including him and the cats, was white, except her.

He draped his clothes with military precision over her white tufted night stand, pulled aside her white velvet bedspread and slipped between her white satin sheets. Lying at attention, he felt as if he should have scrubbed his body for seven minutes with Phisohex and donned a white surgical gown, mask, and cap.

While he stared apprehensively at the pale face looking down apprehensively at him from the mirrored ceiling, she stepped into the doorway of the room, her arms akimbo.

"What about our champagne?" she asked, her eyes flashing humorously.

"I put it in the fridge to cool," he said.

"I want it now. I've chilled some glasses in the freezer."

As he shuffled self-consciously across the thick, white bedroom carpet, she writhed out of her gown and stood awesomely naked before him, her beautifully shaped arms outstretched. The contrast of her dark-brown body with the stark-white surroundings was startling.

They kissed in the doorway. Ten seconds later, she stepped back and said, "Quick, Doctor, the champagne!—I'll be in bed."

"Yes, Ma'am."

In the kitchen, the Siamese cats looked up at him from their dishes, blinked in contempt, and resumed eating. Still trembling from the kiss, he wrestled with the cork on the insufficiently chilled bottle of Möet et Chandon.

With a sharp report, the cork bounced off the ceiling and dropped between the cats, who took off for the bathroom like a pair of 110-meter hurdlers. In their sudden departure, they splattered Purina Cat Chow across the white vinyl floor. Meanwhile, following the cork, almost half the champagne leaped out of the bottle and splattered against the kitchen window.

"Oh, JESUS!" cried the doctor.

She appeared in the kitchen doorway as the doctor was shakily pouring the remainder of the champagne into the glasses.

"What a god-awful mess," she observed, as he handed her a glass.

"Lord knows I tried my best to please you, Miss Katana," he said, in his best Butterfly McQueen impersonation.

"Yes, you did. You picked my cotton, fed my animals, mended my clothes, and slaved over my hot stove."

"But there's one thing, Miss Katana."

"What's that, Butterfly?"

"I don't do floors and windows."

After that, it was a greedy, mutual consumption of champagne, white toast, and caviar—he being the white toast, she the caviar.

22 FRIDAY, MARCH 24, 1978
7:51 P.M. HERRICK HOSPITAL E.R.

After forty-five minutes of frenzied resuscitation, the comatose patient, now naked under a green sheet, was technically alive. His heart was beating on its own, his breathing sustained by the rotund Dr. Weinstein, who still pondered the fate of the pizza that had been delivered just before Dr. Sunshine was wheeled in. Could microwaving possibly revive it? He was willing to try.

The lab tech phoned the E.R. to report the patient's catastrophic blood sugar—twelve milligrams percent.

"Oh my God!" said Dr. Weinstein. "Give him a hundred cc push of 50 percent dextrose. Does anybody know—was Hilly on insulin?"

Nobody knew.

The portable X-rays taken of the patient were being studied by Dr. Noah Epstein, the best radiologist in town, who had almost killed himself racing his Beetle to the hospital after the E.R. secretary phoned him. Three surgeons, also hastily summoned, huddled with the radiologist before the view box. The cadaverous light passing through the gray films bathed the doctors' faces, already paled by the sight of their stricken colleague. The X-ray findings did nothing to improve their complexions.

A piece of bone the size of a silver dollar was missing from the top of the patient's skull, the tip of his fifth dorsal spinous process was gone, his seventh and eighth cervical vertebrae were crushed. ("Oh dear, oh shit, oh dear!" said the neurosurgeon, Dr. A. Henley Edwards, Jr., when he saw the cervical spine films.) A bullet was lodged in the patient's left shoulder, the left humerus was fractured near its head, three right ribs were shattered, and, almost for comic relief, a tiny bone in his left wrist had sustained a partial, hairline fracture.

"Can you see any midline shift?" asked Dr. Edwards, squinting at the skull films.

"Yes," said the radiologist, pointing with the tip of a pencil. "See? Right there."

"Oh dear, oh shit, oh dear!"

Dr. Bernard ("Bubba") Levine, the vascular surgeon, studied the dead-white X-ray image of a dagger protruding from a greatly enlarged spleen and drawled, "Fuuuuck." (Dr. Levine was a Texas Jew.) When the chest film was slapped on the lighted screen, Dr. James Kanamura, the thoracic surgeon, took one look at the harpoon skewering the patient's right lung and sharply sucked in air through his clenched teeth.

"Sssss!"

Along with Dr. Kanamura's inhaled "Sssss," the harpoon elicited Dr. Edwards's mournful, "Oh dear, oh shit, oh dear," and Dr. Levine's contemplative, "Fuuuuck."

The doctors' refrain of "Sssss," "Oh dear, oh shit, oh dear," and "Fuuuuck" was to be repeated in various sequences and frequencies during the five hours they would labor over the patient in the operating room.

Within two hours of Dr. Sunshine's arrival, six pints of blood had been pumped into his veins through the needles Clarinet had inserted. The comatose patient's skin was less clammy. He was now breathing on his own. Having clipped a plastic oxygen tube to the patient's nostrils, Wobbles Weinstein stood in the nurse's station reducing the plump E.R. secretary to tears over the disappearance of his pizza. Her garlic-scented breath betrayed her protestations of innocence.

Dr. Sunshine's blood sugar was now normal. Dr. Edwards had tightly bandaged his scalp wound to stop the profuse bleeding. With his head wrapped in a turban of cotton bunting, the wide-eyed patient resembled a swami in deep meditation.

When Mrs. Sunshine arrived in the E.R., a dozen nurses and doctors were swarming over her husband. The E.R. secretary greeted her with tears and a hug.

"I'm *so* sorry, Mrs. Sunshine."

"But what happened?" she cried.

"Nobody knows."

She tried to force her way to her husband's side. Mr. Devereux intercepted her.

"Mrs. Sunshine, I'm Devereux, the orderly."

"Oh Mr. Devereux," she said, her tear-stained face smiling weakly, "Hilly always spoke so highly of you. How is he? What *happened*?"

"We don't know what happened. And I'm sorry, but he ain't doin' good at all. He's got multiple injuries. He's unconscious and he's in shock. When one of his docs can shake loose, he'll be able to tell you more."

Mrs. Sunshine's knees suddenly failed her. While Devereux helped her to a chair in the waiting room, her mind suddenly flashed on Jacqueline Kennedy in a Dallas hospital. Mr. Devereux gave her a box of Kleenex and found himself reaching for one of the tissues, after she did.

A CAT scan confirmed Dr. Edwards' diagnosis of subdural hematoma; a growing tumor of blood was filling the space between the patient's brain and the inside of his skull. In addition to brain damage, Dr. Edwards was certain that Dr. Sunshine had a mangled spinal cord, as evidenced by the crushed vertebrae on the X-rays and the persistent penile erection—the kind hanged men die with. The erection lifted the green sheet to form a small tent over the patient's pelvis.

Thus, not only was the swami in deep meditation, but he had achieved some degree of levitation as well.

At midnight, Dr. Sunshine—eyes still opened, pupils widely dilated—was wheeled to the O.R. The black perforations in the white acoustic ceiling impinged on the patient's retina as he glided down the corridors. On the darkest night of his life, Dr. Sunshine perceived these visual stimuli as black stars in a white sky.

THE ZODIAC TOUR '76–'77

23 TUESDAY, AUGUST 24, 1976
VIRGO WITH VIRGO

When they first met, the painfully thin Virgin in the white paper gown had been seated cross-legged on the end of his examining table. She opened a notebook on her scrawny lap and looked up at the doctor through granny glasses that diminished the size, but not the luster, of her dark brown eyes.

"I brought a list of my symptoms so I wouldn't forget anything," she said.

"Good," said Dr. Sunshine, lying through his smiling teeth.

She could not have known that when he saw a patient pull out a long list of questions, he wanted to walk out of the room and seal the door with concrete.

When they had laboriously worked through her litany of complaints, he pronounced her diagnosis: severe bulimia. On hearing this, she burst into tears, jumped to her feet, and allowed her bony chest to be cradled in his powerful arms. Through her paper gown, he counted twenty-four delicate ribs plus two promising breasts.

"Roast beef! Mashed potatoes! Gravy!" ordered the doctor into the hollow behind her right clavicle. "And keep it all down!"

"You mean I'll have to give up my 'scarf-and-barf' diet?" she asked, nibbling his earlobe.

After three more office visits, her burgeoning figure reached momentary perfection along its inexorable course towards obesity. At the same time, their mutual lust also blossomed.

When he popped the question, the cautious Virgin suggested they meet at a motel. She didn't want to arouse her husband's suspicions by having him find her at home in bed with her internist.

Dr. Sunshine was not at all happy about a motel rendezvous, but his practice was not overly populated with Virgins at the time—especially perfectly built ones. He agreed to meet her at the Wanderlust Inn, near the Oakland Coliseum, early one evening at the end of the following week.

The motel lobby was housed in one of those all-purpose glass and stucco California buildings that interchangeably serve as nursing homes, motels, and mortuaries. After a short but painful transaction, the unctuous, silver-haired clerk, a mortician manqué, handed Dr. Sunshine the key to Room 298C.

"Thank you, Mr. Hirschfield," said the clerk. "I hope your stay with us will be a restful one."

"You can never tell," said Dr. Sunshine, who had taken the precaution of assuming the name of Leon Hirschfield and the occupation of manufacturer's representative.

Behind its versatile facade, the Wanderlust Inn stretched endlessly in all directions. A rat's maze of dimly lit corridors and stairways connected its three hundred rooms in four separate buildings. With a bottle of Schramsberg champagne held in one arm and the supple waist of his Virgin in the other, Dr. Sunshine made a crucial wrong turn, as was his wont, and they ended up walking the entire circumference of the motel complex before arriving at the door of Room 298C.

"I see you chose the Great Circle Route," she said.

"Don't rub it in," he said, fumbling with the key and latch.

"Relax," she said. "This is supposed to be fun. It's a good thing I brought along my massage oils."

"Rub it in," he said, finally getting the door to open.

Since Virgo was their common sun sign, they each undressed meticulously and laid out their clothes to resemble a window at Sak's.

"There!" they said simultaneously, turning to size up each other's bodies. By this time, each was a little on the heavy side, but there was no turning back now.

"Your shoulder muscles are like a hunk of wood—a yoke," she said, as they embraced. "Lie down on your stomach and I'll try to loosen you up."

With a clear amber oil that gave off a light scent of sandalwood, she massaged his trapezius muscles. He groaned in ecstasy as her insistent fingers turned his wooden yoke to hard rubber, then hard rubber to soft wax. After fifteen minutes, she had kneaded into submission every muscle on the back of his body. He had almost dozed off when she bent down and whispered into his ear, "Now turn over, babe."

He was amazed at how heavy his body felt as he obeyed her, so reluctant were his massaged muscles to budge. Working on his flip side, her seemingly boneless hands glided over his chest, arms, abdomen, and legs. In transit, her fingertips lightly grazed Poindexter.

Thanks to her exertions, the doctor's body fairly glistened with balm, and hers, with a dew of perspiration. "Darling," she murmured, "I'm thirsty. Let's take a champagne break."

Receiving a nod of approval from Poindexter, he slipped out of bed and picked up the bottle of Schramsberg from the floor of the closet. Chilled when he had bought it, the champagne had developed a mild fever in the body-heated room.

"Ice," said the doctor. "There's no ice in this crummy room."

"I saw an ice machine down the hall," she said.

"Which direction?" he asked.

Languidly, she pointed a waving finger at the door.

"I'm not quite sure," she said. "Try taking a left when you're out the door—you can't miss it."

He walked back to the bed, bent over, and kissed the top of her head.

"I'll be right back."

"Hadn't you better cover up a bit?"

"I can't. I don't want to grease up my clothes or the towels. Here, I'll use this."

Over Poindexter, he clamped a cardboard ice bucket labeled, "Wanderlust Inn." She roared with laughter as he said, "Look—a complimentary codpiece. I'll just be a sec."

As he made for the door, she quoted a line from My Fair Lady: *"Oozing charm from every pore, he oiled his way across the floor."*

He stepped into the brightly lit corridor and looked for miles in either direction without seeing another soul or an ice machine. He turned left and set off briskly. Twenty-five feet ahead, a door to one of the rooms opened and what appeared to be a nuclear family of four stepped into the corridor. Before they spotted him, he dashed down a stairwell and soon found himself in another infinity of corridors.

He proceeded to tramp over a Sahara of beige nylon carpeting in search of ice—a wandering Jew with a cardboard bucket guarding his circumcision. And then—was it a mirage?—a bulky white appliance peeked out of a service area a hundred paces ahead. Ice! With a metal scoop, he filled his bucket to the brim with mini-cubes. Hesitating, he turned to find his way back.

He was lost. A chicken with its head cut off had a keener sense of direction than did Dr. Sunshine, tracer of lost Virgins. What is more, one could forgive a headless chicken for not rembering where it roosted, but what was his *excuse for forgetting his room number? Through the years, on the innumerable occasions of his getting lost, he had always depended on the kindness of strangers, but what stranger would take kindly to being approached by a naked man holding an ice bucket?*

After twenty minutes of frantically dodging guests and searching for his room, he heard the sound of goal-oriented footsteps rapidly closing from the rear. Turning, he spied a beefy, uniformed guard, his gun drawn, bearing down on him.

In a last-ditch effort at covering up, he plunged Poindexter into the bucket of half-melted ice, much as a Chinese waiter does with a warm, honey-glazed banana before serving it.

"All right, buddy," said the security guard. "I'm taking you down to the office and calling the police."

The guard grabbed an oiled arm which abruptly slipped out of his grasp.

"Don't try to squirm away!" he shouted. "I'll shoot!"

"I'm not trying to squirm away—I'm a guest here."

"What's your room number?"

"That's the problem; I've forgotten it for the moment. But if you simply call down and ask the clerk where Mr. Leon Hirschfield is staying, I'll be eternally grateful."

With a gun pointed at his shiny back, Dr. Sunshine was marched to the nearest stairwell where, to his immense relief, they bumped into his Virgin. She was fully dressed and appeared fit to be tied.

"Wait!" said Dr. Sunshine. "Darling, tell him who I am."

"I never saw this man before in my life," she said, deadpan, then broke into a smile. "Only kidding—this is my friend, Dr. Sunshine. Where've you been, Hilly?"

"But he said his name was Hirschfield!" cried the guard, grabbing the doctor's arm, which again eluded his grasp.

"Hirschfield is the name I gave the clerk," said Dr. Sunshine. "I don't like to advertise that I'm a doctor when I stay at a motel. They might call me out on a case."

"Oh, I see," said the guard, replacing his gun in its holster. "What's in the bucket, Doc, your instruments?"

Back in the room with his fellow Virgo, the doctor put the champagne on ice and wrapped Poindexter in a hot washcloth. To kill time, Dr. Sunshine inserted a quarter into a slot, activating the bed vibrator. For fifteen minutes, the two Virgins sat up and jerkily watched the seven o'clock news, an expe-rience Dr. Sunshine likened to viewing an in-flight movie while passing through mild turbulence.

When they opened the Schramsberg and unwrapped Poindexter, the Vir-gin mused, "I wonder if they served champagne at the unveiling of the Washington Monument."

After she annointed Poindexter with some more of her bewitching balm, Sunshine drew her down alongside him. The next twenty minutes were an enactment of Hart Crane's rapturous lines:

> *Bunched in mutual glee*
> *—o murmurless and shined*
> *In oilrinsed circles*
> *of blind ecstasy!*

Afterward, they lay side by side like a pair of spent, greased Channel swimmers. For ten minutes, the only sound in the room was a faint gurgling from their stomachs.

"Cheeseburgers," he finally whispered into her ear.

"French fries," she moaned, licking her lips.

Simultaneously, they both clenched their bodies and gasped, "Chocolate shakes!"

24 SATURDAY, MARCH 25, 1978
12:30 A.M. HERRICK HOSPITAL

"What you got there?" asked Orderly Devereux.

"Oh, not much," said Nurse Clarinet as he riffled the pages of a small black leather volume. "Just Dr. Sunshine's appointment book."

The young nurse and the middle-aged orderly sipped warm Scotch from plastic medication cups as they sat in Devereux's cluttered lit-tle office off the basement laundry room. It was 12:33 A.M., half an hour after Dr. Sunshine had been wheeled to the O.R.

"How'd you get that?" asked Mr. Devereux.

"Easy. While I was cutting away the doctor's jacket, I found it in-side his left breast pocket. See the hole in the middle? I think this book stopped the arrow Parnell mentioned."

"Let me see," said Mr. Devereux.

Mr. Clarinet handed over the notebook.

"Looks like a lotta names and numbers is all," said Mr. Devereux.

"Yes, but chances are those names and numbers include some of the creeps who tried to kill him. Only your closest friends or your family would go to that much trouble to bump you off."

"Yeah, when I was five, my brother George tried to flush me down the toilet, head first."

"You know, my hairdresser charges me twelve bucks for essentially the same experience," said Mr. Clarinet. "Come on, Dev, let's use my car. Your El Dorado always draws a patrol car."

"Where we goin'?"

"To Dr. Sunshine's office."

"What for?"

"To play with his computer."

25 SATURDAY, MARCH 25, 1978
12:43 A.M. DR. SUNSHINE'S OFFICE

It was a ten-minute ride from Herrick Hospital on Dwight Way to Dr. Sunshine's office on Prince Street, near Alta Bates. By socioeconomic measurements, the distance between the two hospitals—Herrick and Alta Bates—was much greater than a ten-minute ride. Between the black wino dying of alcoholic hepatitis in Herrick and the WASP "social drinker" dying of "liver failure" in Alta Bates—between muscatel and the martini—lay a yawning, farting, belching chasm on whose either trembling brink swayed a man, staring with a jaundiced eye into the fetid abyss.

Cheers.

Enroute, having bypassed the fetid abyss by turning left on Bryant, Mr. Clarinet's white Honda Civic was the only moving car in South Berkeley.

The dimly lit parking garage beneath the stucco building on Prince Street was empty. Mr. Clarinet drove past the space marked "Dr. Sunshine" and parked in the darkest corner of the garage.

Led by Mr. Clarinet, the two men walked around to the west side of the building, where the top of a neighboring fence afforded easy access to the small deck off Dr. Sunshine's second-floor office. As a patient of Dr. Sunshine himself, Mr. Clarinet was no stranger to the premises. As a former inmate of the Santa Rita Correctional Facility for Men, Mr. Devereux was no stranger to breaking and entering. The two men pulled on latex surgical gloves.

After Mr. Devereux had deftly lifted one panel of the sliding glass door off its track, they stepped into Dr. Sunshine's rear examining room. Handsomely decorated by Mrs. Sunshine with framed copies of Cezanne prints, straw Mexican mobiles, and Danish lounge chairs, the large room almost achieved the intended ambience of a study in a private residence. The only patently clinical fixture was the sleek, walnut and green-leather examining table. It was partially covered with a white rectangle of paper freshly dimpled by the ample buttocks of Hattie Jackson, Dr. Sunshine's last patient.

The two men crept toward the sound of a Mozart string quartet at the far end of the office. A Sony portable radio tuned to KDFC was gamely serving as Dr. Sunshine's anti-burglar device when Mr. Devereux turned it off. (As a deterrent to crime, Mozart was a bust.)

Mr. Clarinet stepped into the front business office. He lit an unfiltered Pall Mall and sat down at the North Star computer that served as the nerve center of the small retail business known as Hillel I. Sunshine, M.D., Inc. (On the advice of his accountant, Dr. Sunshine had incorporated himself three years before, when his net income exceeded one hundred thousand dollars for the first time.)

"What're you doin', Clar?"

Mr. Clarinet's fingers flew over the computer's keyboard, lighting up the video screen with a density of data.

"I'm hunting for the doctor's assassins," said Mr. Clarinet, staring intently at the opened appointment book.

"Look at this, Dev. On the last page, just above this little rip made by the arrow, I found the word 'Zodiac,' followed by seven digits. I tried dialing them on the phone at Herrick and got nowhere. Then I remembered how Dr. Sunshine liked to show off his office computer. I thought I'd try feeding these digits into his North Star."

"Where'd you learn to work one of them things? I didn' know you was into computers."

"I'm not. Steven is. My roommate. He's teaching me on his Apple."

In response to Clarinet's key-punching, the video screen suddenly went blank, then flashed the words, RUN ZODIAC, and underneath, ENTER CODE.

Clarinet glanced at the appointment book and punched in the numbers, 9123513.

INCORRECT CODE, scolded the computer. Then Clarinet reversed the digits. INCORRECT CODE. After trying a dozen other variations, he absently punched in every other digit, whereupon the computer emitted an approving beep and asked, WHICH SUN SIGN?

Clarinet looked up in wide-blue-eyed triumph at Devereux and then typed, RUN ARIES.

GRAPHIC OR BIO? asked the computer.

GRAPHIC, replied Clarinet.

Obediently the computer displayed on its screen a brilliantly colored picture of Dr. Sunshine and a redheaded woman demonstrating the missionary position in a gaily quilted bed. Of almost photographic realism, the picture had been originally sketched with a copper-tipped pen on a computer-linked graphics tablet. Obviously derivative, the illustration owed its style both to the eighteenth century's Utamaro and the twentieth century's Vargas. In the picture, Dr. Sunshine wore a kimono (Utamaro); the woman did not (Vargas).

After five seconds, the picture dissolved in a cascade of falling colors resembling spent fireworks.

Beep went the computer.

"*Shee-it,*" said Mr. Devereux.

"Good God," said Mr. Clarinet.

GRAPHIC OR BIO? asked the computer, again.

BIO, answered Clarinet with trembling fingers.

The screen lit up with the following data:

V.L. Aries.
D.O.B. 3/25/45. HT. 5'1". WT. 102.

HAIR: Red. EYES: Green. VITAL STATS: 37/21/36.
OCCUP.: Paralegal Asst. RULING PLANET: Mars.
PSYCHE: Nag Nag Nag. RESPONSE: Multi Orgasmic
after ½ hr. 4play. PRFRD. POSITION: Missnry.
STYLE: Moves to Left Good. MAJOR FLAW: Mildewed
Towels in Guest Bthrm. BRTHSTN: Aqmrn. PRFM: Chn
#5 &/or Charlie. CMPSR: Mzrt. AUTH: Hmngwy.
DRINK: Hrvy. Wlbngr. FOOD: Lv. Mn. Lbstr.

"Dev," said Clarinet, "go to the doctor's filing cabinet and pull the chart of a patient whose initials are V. L. and whose date of birth is 3/25/45."

"And who moves to the left good," said Devereux, emitting a falsetto *hee-hee* and shaking his head. "Oh, Doctah Sunshine, you was somethin' else!"

Forty-five minutes later, Clarinet and Devereux had twelve of Dr. Sunshine's clinical charts stacked on the desk. Nothing in the contents of the charts hinted that the doctor had anything but a clinical interest in the twelve patients. Their progress notes recounted boring episodes of bronchitis, cystitis, muscle sprains, and sore throats—the staples of the primary care physician. One of the charts alluded to testicular feminization, another, to Wilson's disease.

"Listen to this," said Clarinet. "The final note in V. L.'s chart: '4/20/76. Referred to Dr. Horowitz for psychotherapy.' Funny it doesn't mention what her problem was."

"Hey," said Devereux, "here's the same thing in R. T.'s chart: '5/21/76. Referred to Dr. Horowitz for psychotherapy.' That's all it says."

In fact, the final entry in each of the twelve charts was identical, only the dates differing.

Clarinet and Devereux briefly scanned the computerized BIO and GRAPHIC data on each woman, pausing only to gape from time to time. Then Clarinet typed the names of the twelve patients on a piece of scrap paper and jumped to his feet.

"Hurry up, Dev," he said, heading for the back of the office. "You know how shrinks hate to be kept waiting."

THE ZODIAC TOUR '76–'77

26 SATURDAY, SEPTEMBER 25, 1976
LIBRA WITH VIRGO

When the pleasingly zaftig cellist opened the door for him, the rich sound of a Mozart opera, the garlicky aroma of a simmering clam sauce, and the intriguing sight of her full figure undulating within her burgundy gown, overwhelmed him. Her face was flushed from having just drained boiling water off the linguine.

"How nice—Don Giovanni," *said the doctor.*

"It takes one to know one," *she said, opening her arms and clutching his bottle of Chianti Classico against one breast and him against the other. Under the folds of her gown, her surprisingly slim waist, he noted, formed a narrow isthmus between her Atlantic breasts and Pacific hips.*

"For a change, your timing is perfect," *she said.* The pasta is al dente, the sauce is ready, the bread's warm, and I've just laid the last anchovy on the salad."

"Ah, lucky anchovy," *said the doctor.* "How contented he looks lying on that lettuce leaf. So brown and oiled—like my Uncle Morrie, sunning himself on a green towel at Miami Beach."

"Why don't you open the Chianti, darling? I'll serve you in a sec."

"But aren't you joining me?" *he asked, noting that only one place had been set on her dining table.*

"Yes, sweetheart, but not for lunch. I'm on a diet, remember? If you don't mind, I'd like you to try cutting me down to size in bed."

"Look," *he said, as she poured the clam sauce over his linguine,* "it'll probably take me fifteen minutes to eat two thousand calories here. Do you know how long it would take to burn off the same number in bed?"

"Yes—five hours and thirty-two minutes. Exactly the duration of the nine symphonies of Beethoven on Deutsche Grammophon. You told me on the phone you had the whole afternoon off—wife at Tahoe with the kids, you said."

"The nine symphonies of Beethoven!" *he wailed.* "There's no conductor on earth who could hold up his baton that long."

"That's not what I've heard about you guys in your forties."

"Look, you're talking to a man who couldn't make it through Bolero in his twenties."

"We'll continue this interesting discussion after lunch. Eat hearty, my lad. I've got to load the record changer." She motioned toward the bedroom. "While you're eating, I'll be in the orchestra pit, tuning up."

The Italian dishes before him suddenly turned into mandolins; he picked at his food. At length, the melancholy conductor rose from the table and edged toward the bedroom. Supine on her Sealy Posturepedic mattress, with one shapely, pink leg bent at the knee, the Libran was living proof of Sunshine's highly controversial maxim that a full-figured woman, no matter how plump, always looks good lying on her back.

The First Symphony, to his surprise, went quite well, although he kept trying to exceed the tempo of the lovely Andante of the second movement.

"Not so fast, maestro," she cooed into his ear. "Remember, the First Symphony marks the transition from eighteenth century Classicism to the Romanticism of the nineteenth. So take it easy till the third movement—then sock it to me."

Done.

Next, they managed to thrash their way through the Second Symphony without mishap. During the enchanting Larghetto, he remarked that with the piddling exception of Bolero, this was his first experience with hard-core phonography.

The "Eroica" posed some problems, especially when a screeching noise interrupted the Scherzo of the third movement.

"What happened?" he panted.

"I think the needle slipped out of the groove."

"Like hell it has!" he said, increasing his tempo.

"No, idiot, I mean on the record."

"Oh."

While she changed the record, seductively lowering the round disc over the metal rod, she informed him that the Fourth Symphony, coming up, had reminded Robert Schumann of "a slender Greek maiden lying between two northern giants."

"I never would have guessed Robert Schumann went to that kind of party," he said.

Having crushed the slender maiden between them, Maestro Sunshine and *his one-woman orchestra braced themselves for the four hammer blows that open the Fifth Symphony. As they sounded, he pounded them home.*

Flushing a deep rose, she cried, "Ohhh!"

"Quite a release, huh?" he said.

"Yes, it's Deutsche Grammophon with von Karajan, but frankly, it's a toss-up between that and the budget release by Victrola with Charles Munch."

"I'm not referring to that kind of release," he said, petulantly slapping her thigh.

After the exhausting tempo of the Fifth, the Pastorale seemed to them like an escape from downtown San Francisco to the vineyards of Napa Valley. During the Pastorale, their lovemaking became lyrical, almost bucolic— rather, he imagined, like a soft roll in the hay.

The doctor was decidedly up for the Seventh Symphony, his personal favorite. After tapping his baton against her podium to indicate his readiness, he drove her as relentlessly as von Karajan astride the Berlin Philharmonic, and elicited sounds from her just as rapturous.

"Bravo!" she gasped, as the last note sounded.

At the conductor's insistence, his concertmaster, Poindexter, stood up and took a little bow.

Halfway through the Eighth Symphony, having almost shot his bolt during the Seventh, the doctor came close to throwing in the towel. Their mutual perspiration had caused his body to begin hydroplaning over hers, his lower back muscles were in constant spasm, his breathing had become stertorous and his knees were a mass of sheet burns, and yet . . . and yet again, he pressed on, right through the light-hearted fourth movement of the Eighth.

After four-and-a-half hours of sustained Beethoven, he had conducted himself brilliantly. And now he faced the monumental Ninth with its ecstatic choral rendition of Schiller's "Ode to Joy." He was not at all sure he could sustain his libido throughout a creative effort that had always inspired in him reverence and awe.

To his surprise, and hers, the first three movements were an audioerotic romp. They had by now ceased to be conductor and orchestra; they had become one with the music, one with the instruments. He bowed her cello, she tootled his flute. The slick surfaces of their bodies shone like brass, clashed together like cymbals. Their throats emitted French horny blasts, clarinet wails, oboe bleats, bassoonoid groans, reedy cries.

When, finally, the bass-baritone erupted with, "O freunde, nicht diese Tone!" she clenched her body and climaxed, her pubococcygeus muscle thrumming like the G string on a bass fiddle. He could barely contain himself, but was able to hold out until the middle of the soprano solo, "Ich non haben Befriedigung," when he experienced an orgasm that rose up from the smallest bones of his feet and did not quit until his skull rattled.

All passion spent, he fell back alongside his supine Libran and let the music carry off his remains.

"Oh, Hillel, you can't quit now. We haven't finished the Ninth yet."

"Ach!" he said, throwing his right arm over his eyes. "The heartbreak of premature ejaculation!"

When the symphony ended, she lumbered into the bathroom, then skipped out to announce, "Congratulations, Doctor. I've lost almost nine pounds!"

"Ah, that's nothing!" he said. "Next veek ve do der complete Ring Cycle. Zixteen pounds, I guarantee it!"

27 SATURDAY, MARCH 25, 1978
2:00 A.M. DR. HOROWITZ'S OFFICE

Clarinet and Devereux tiptoed up the front steps of the small redwood office building on Walnut Street in North Berkeley. A converted private home, the office of Samuel K. Horowitz, M.D., Inc. emanated a woodsy coziness. Through the front window, the pale blue, flickering glow of a TV set added a touch of domesticity almost as warm as the glint of firelight.

Devereux quietly jimmied the front door lock, and the two men slipped into Dr. Horowitz's darkened consultation room. As they suspected, the doctor was in.

Sipping Dom Perignon from a Waterford tulip glass, the psychiatrist was seated on a Brazilian lounge chair before a fifty-inch Sony TV screen. Softly, the two intruders sat down behind him on a black leather couch.

Illuminating the screen before them was the unmistakable image of

Dr. Sunshine, sans kimono this time, and that of an unclad, fair-skinned woman, disporting themselves aerobically on a black leather couch. The woman's heart-shaped face did not resemble that of any of the twelve computerized portraits Clarinet and Devereux had studied a short time before in Sunshine's office.

Dr. Horowitz pushed a button, freezing the couple on the screen just at the point when they appeared to be either enjoying a mutual orgasm or suffering from simultaneously pulled back muscles.

Dr. Horowitz put down his glass and stuck a True cigarette in his mouth. Mr. Devereux leaned forward with his Zippo and lit it.

Dr. Horowitz coughed, screamed, and leaped to his feet. The Sony projected garish flesh tones onto his white, Guatemalan shirt.

"Who's there?" he rasped.

"Two friends of Dr. Sunshine," said Mr. Clarinet.

Dr. Horowitz bolted for the door. Mr. Devereux tackled him cleanly. Lacking a football helmet, the psychiatrist suffered a minor concussion when his head struck the side of a teak wastebasket. Mr. Clarinet flipped on the overhead light and turned off the VCR. The spacious, wood-paneled room glittered with Oriental antiques.

After they hustled the balding, bearded psychiatrist into a supine position on his black leather couch, Mr. Clarinet employed some minor resuscitative techniques to bring him around. While Mr. Devereux held his switchblade under the doctor's beard, Mr. Clarinet switched on the TV camera mounted in the bookcase facing the couch.

"All right now, Dr. Horowitz," said Mr. Clarinet, "let's try some free association. Tell me the first thing that comes to your mind. What do you know about the attempted assassination of Dr. Hillel Sunshine?"

"Attempted?" mumbled Dr. Horowitz, fighting off the effects of champagne and concussion.

"Are these ladies your patients?" asked Mr. Clarinet, handing him the typewritten list of twelve names.

Still groggy, Dr. Horowitz squinted through his gold-rimmed glasses and said, "Yes, I believe so."

"Who referred these women to you?" asked Mr. Clarinet.

"Hilly Sunshine," said the psychiatrist, blanching.

"What was troubling them, doctor?"

"Hilly Sunshine," said the psychiatrist.

"How so?" asked Mr. Clarinet.

"When he was finished with them, Hilly sent me all his women."

"What for?"

"Debriefing."

"Who was that lady with Dr. Sunshine up there on the TV?" asked Mr. Devereux.

"That was no lady," said Dr. Horowitz, "that was my wife."

28 SATURDAY, MARCH 25, 1978
5:30 A.M. HERRICK HOSPITAL

"The patient tolerated the procedure well and was taken to the Recovery Room in stable condition." This is how the report of Dr. Sunshine's operation ended. Dictated by Dr. Edwards and signed by him, Dr. Kanamura, and Dr. Levine, it ran to seven single-spaced, typewritten pages. It spoke of retraction, ligation, drainage, suction, resection, dissection, extraction of foreign bodies, reduction of fractures, multiple transfusion, and finally of suturing and dressing, and the obligatory sign-off: "The patient tolerated the procedure well and was taken to the Recovery Room in stable condition." (Translation: The operation was a bloody mess and when the surgeons ran out of things to do, it was a toss-up whether the patient should be sent to the morgue or the Recovery Room; for the sake of appearances, he was sent to the Recovery Room.)

Dr. Sunshine had had his entire blood volume replaced three times during the operation, he had remained comatose, his heart had stopped beating once, his spleen and half his right lung had been removed, he was no longer breathing on his own, he had gone into profound shock three times, but otherwise he had "tolerated the procedure well."

Dr. Edwards had seen the bruised, swollen surface of the patient's brain, had touched the bloody stalk of his upper spinal cord, and concluded after the lengthy procedure that he and his fellow surgeons could now safely transfer the patient to the care of a botanist.

29 SATURDAY, MARCH 25, 1978
2:10 A.M. DR. HOROWITZ'S OFFICE

"Your wife?" asked Mr. Clarinet.

"Actually, my former wife," said Dr. Samuel Horowitz, lighting another cigarette. The psychiatrist lay back on his couch, stifled a burp and crossed his legs.

"What happened to her?" asked Mr. Devereux.

"She left me," said Dr. Horowitz, his eyes suddenly brimming with tears.

"When?" asked Mr. Clarinet.

"The same night I showed her the video tape of Sunshine humping her on this very couch."

"How did you catch them in the act?" asked Mr. Clarinet.

"Accidentally. I use a hidden TV camera for playback therapy and forgot to turn it off before I left."

"You showed her the tape?" said Mr. Clarinet. "That must have wiped her out."

"You don't know my wife. After their TV performance reached its climax, we just sat there in our bedroom in the dark, smoking grass and not saying anything. After five minutes, her slow, husky voice came out of the darkness and said, 'Play it again, Sam.'"

"Did you?" asked Mr. Clarinet.

"No. Those were her last words of our marriage. I opened a drawer, handed my wife her vibrator and said, 'Buzz off.'" Those were *my* last words."

"Well, at least you had the last word."

"Yes, but not the last laugh—until tonight."

"What do you mean?" asked Mr. Devereux.

"Seeing my twelve little creeps circle Sunshine's car and destroy him was the peak experience of my life. I was right here watching the traffic report on Channel 8 and suddenly there they were. I was waiting for a news bulletin of what happened and instead, I got the assassination live!"

Dr. Horowitz dried his tears with the back of his hand and smiled fondly.

"Your twelve little creeps?" said Mr. Clarinet.

"Yes. Sunshine's dirty dozen. He sent me one a month for a year. Each one a basket case. All of 'em needed long-term therapy—it was a nightmare for me. Without exception, his twelve rejected lovers had each been abused as a child by her father or stepfather or an uncle. Oh, Sunshine knew how to pick 'em! This kind of girl grows up to be a young woman that a middle-aged man can readily pull into bed—but just let him try to kick her out!

"I was still treating the women individually, when I caught Sunshine and my wife *in flagrante delicto*—oh, did my *wife* have an uncle! After I sent her packing, I persuaded each of Sunshine's jilted Jezebels to join a women's group of twelve. I assured each one that the others were also suffering from an overexposure to Sunshine. Once we got together, I merely helped them bring about a collective cure.

"I confided in them—I told them what Sunshine had done to my wife—and how I felt about it. They pledged me their undying loyalty.

"A cult was born: The Sunshine Girls. We spent a year sharing our common hatred and working out the details of our revenge. As their guru, I used only a minimum of mushrooms and a modest dose of hypnotherapy to change them from discarded lovers to avenging demons. In the end, I was able to unleash against Sunshine the fury of a woman scorned, to the twelfth power! No man could survive that."

"You don't know Doctah Sunshine," said Devereux, pressing the tip of his blade into Dr. Horowitz's curly dewlap. The psychiatrist evasively snapped his head back, and in so doing, lost his beard. Devereux and Clarinet stared at the frizzy brown pelt dangling from the end of the knife.

"Whoops," said Mr. Devereux.

"Why the fake beard, doctor?" asked Mr. Clarinet.

"For the same reason I sport an ersatz Jewish beak. The plastic surgeon in Rio couldn't believe I wanted my perfect Aryan nose lengthened and hooked. I also had myself circumcised. What's more, at my insistence, Dr. Concepción used the excised tissue as a skin graft for the phony bald spot on my crown—a case of robbing peter to pay poll, wouldn't you say? Is it any wonder my scalp tingles whenever I'm near a beautiful woman? And look at my hair—would you believe it was straight and blonde before I had it dyed brunette and set in a natural?'

"You certainly had *me* fooled," said Mr. Clarinet.

"As for my regulation psychiatric beard, I found it easier to buy one than to grow one. Under these granny glasses, I wear brown contacts over my blue eyes."

"What are you tryin' to hide, Doctah Ho'witz?" asked Mr. Devereux.

"For one thing, my real name: Werner von Mundt. For another, my background. I'm the son of an SS officer, a concentration camp commandant, who was executed for war crimes.

"When I was twelve, I learned what he had done from a schoolmate. I was in shock. My mother had told me he was killed in combat at Stalingrad.

"I couldn't understand what had turned my father into a monster. *I had to figure him out.* At the same time, I vowed to repudiate everything he stood for. I grew up with a burning desire to be a Jewish psychiatrist. Freud became for me what Hitler had been for my father. Gentlemen, you are looking at the first Aryan to add a Jew to the world—himself.

"In order to complete my impersonation of a Jewish psychiatrist, I, of course, married a blonde shiksa. Frankly, I would have preferred a Jewess."

"Good grief," said Mr. Clarinet, "a closet goy!"

"Precisely," said Dr. Horowitz, née Mundt. "The Sunshine Girls shared your amazement when I confessed my true identity, but they eventually came to accept me for what I am—my father's son." Tears welled in Dr. Horowitz's eyes. "Even by Berkeley standards, I'm one screwed up shrink, no?"

"Why're you tellin' us all this?" asked Mr. Devereux.

"I don't know—maybe it's the confessional impulse a psychiatrist's couch inspires. Maybe it's because I want to tell *somebody* that when Sunshine seduced my wife, he not only made me a cuckold, but also the last thing I wanted to be—an anti-Semite."

"So you tried to even the score—*subtract* one Jew from the world," said Mr. Clarinet.

"No, his being Jewish wasn't what destroyed him. Sunshine's fatal flaw was his loss of control, his abuse of sexual power—his failure to gain mastery over Poindexter, his phallus. The case of Dr. Sunshine and his alter ego, Poindexter, supports my theory that, in the affairs of men throughout history, the penis, gentlemen, is mightier than the sword."

30 SATURDAY, MARCH 25, 1978
2:30 A.M. HERRICK HOSPITAL I.C.U.

Dreams of a dying doctor:

. . . *peep* . . . *peep* . . . *peep* . . . The five-year-old boy pauses at the top of the stairs to glance at the unopened Sunday paper on the telephone stool. *The Pittsburgh Press*—ponderous, thick, opaque. On the outside, it's "Dick Tracy" in color, protecting "The Katzenjammer Kids" and "Wash Tubs" inside. Bending over, he sniffs the printer's ink and cheap paper—the body odor of his heroes.

. . . *peep* . . . *peep* . . . The canary in the kitchen is hungry. A heavy rhythmic squeak in the hallway—his grandmother is up. He runs down the steps and out the front door of the brick duplex into the crisp morning air. He crashes through the red and yellow leaves carpeting the street and crunches on to the narrow park. He sits on the cold rim of the fountain and stares at the marble cupid with the ugly brown rust stain on its chin.

. . . *peep* . . . *peep* . . . An agitated sparrow, perched on the smooth, white shoulder of cupid's mother, is chirping at her to wipe the chocolate off the kid's face. The mother is giving the sparrow the cold shoulder. ("That's a good one, Hilly.")

. . . *peep* . . . *peep-peep* . . . *peep* . . . "Hillel, hold still! Not another peep out of you!" The rough, cold, wet, mildewed washrag abrades his lips and chin . . . *peep* . . . *peep* . . .

"What *is* this?" thought Dr. Sunshine, emerging from his nostalgic reverie. "Post-coital *tristesse*? It must be—Poindexter feels tumescent, and I'm exhausted. In fact, I can't move. I can't speak! I can't see! This is *not* post-coital *tristesse*. This is coma! I can barely hear the peeping of a monitor . . . My God, I'm in a hospital bed . . . Safe at last! ('Dr. Sunshine won't be able to see you today; he's in a coma.') . . . *peep . . . peep-peep-peep . . . peep . . .*

"Christ, those are extra systoles. Probably ventricular . . . "

"Code Blue, Bed Four! It's Dr. Sunshine!" Peep-peep-peep . . . *peep-peep—eeeeeeeee—*

"What's all the excitement? Somebody's pressing on my chest. Oh God, I'm a dead man—I've never seen such a pure white light . . .

"Look at me down there. So naked without my glasses. So *pale*. Poor baby."

His elan vital, his once-blithe spirit, was hovering just above his body, on hummingbird wings, trying to decide whether to go back in or fly away.

"Jesus, I'm quadriplegic, comatose. Where are my glasses? Oh God, I wish they'd get off my case. What the hell, call it a life. I don't want to go back in there. I can see everything . . . crushed cervical cord . . . punctured lung . . . fibrillating heart . . . hopeless . . .

"Stand back—I'm gonna zap 'im" . . . *eeeeeeeeee—Peep-peep-peep . . . peep . . . peep . . . peep . . .*

"Those idiots! They got my heart beating again . . .

"May Day! May Day! I'm going in . . . "

On hummingbird wings his spirit reentered his body.

"Trapped again. . . . Oh boy. There's only one thing to do in here: Physician, heal thyself."

✪ ✪ ✪

"Oh Hilly! My poor, poor darling! What have they done to you? It's Gloria, my darling. I'm here. You're going to be all right, Hilly. You just *have* to be. They wouldn't let me come to you till now, and they say I can only stay for a few minutes, but I'll be back. Oh Hilly, don't die. I love you so much!"

31 SATURDAY, MARCH 25, 1978
2:40 A.M. DR. HOROWITZ'S OFFICE

"Where are your twelve ladies hiding out tonight?" asked Mr. Clarinet.

"They're not hiding out," said the psychiatrist. "They're dining out. At Denny's in Emeryville." Dr. Horowitz glanced down at his digital watch. "Two-forty. I suspect they've finished their steak and eggs and are about ready to come home to Poppa for dessert."

"What's for dessert?" asked Mr. Devereux.

"A special cake to commemorate Dr. Hillel Sunshine. I baked it myself. I was inspired by the Mexican tradition, on the Day of the Dead, of eating confections shaped and decorated to resemble the naked Jesus."

Dr. Horowitz motioned toward a large cardboard box sitting on his desk. "See for yourself," he said.

Mr. Clarinet walked over to the desk and opened the box to reveal an uncanny, three-foot likeness of Dr. Sunshine in cake and pink icing. The edible internist was naked except for his aviator glasses.

"What did you use for his hair?" asked Mr. Clarinet, in frank admiration.

"Chocolate sprinkles," said Dr. Horowitz, smiling modestly.

"We're sorry to spoil your party, doctor," said Mr. Clarinet, "but your colleague, Dr. Sunshine, is still alive. Your female SWAT team struck out."

Dr. Horowitz's face reddened.

"I *knew* I should have been there!" he said, momentarily losing his American accent. "Killing is *man's* work. I should have *known* Sunshine's whores would screw up when the chips were down."

"Smile, doctor, you're on Candid Camera," said Mr. Clarinet, unloading the cassette from the TV camera and placing it in the VCR.

Mr. Devereux pressed the palm of his hand down on the doctor's bald spot, restraining the psychiatrist's efforts to jump up from his couch.

Devereux and Clarinet started at the sound of boots on the hardwood floor of Dr. Horowitz's outer office. The doctor seized their moment of distraction to lunge for Mr. Devereux's right wrist. As he felt his knife fall to the floor, Devereux instinctively brought his left fist around in a powerful hook to the psychiatrist's jaw. Dr. Horowitz fell back on the couch, unconscious. Devereux and Clarinet scrambled behind the couch just as the door to Dr. Horowitz's consultation room burst open, admitting twelve animated women.

"Oh *there* you are, Werner," said one of the women. "Look at him, ladies—blotto from champagne. No wonder he told us to run along to Denny's. He had some serious drinking to do."

"Oh wow!" said another woman, tilting up the cardboard box. "Dig this wild cake."

A sound of general merriment and wonder swept the room.

"Katana, break out the champagne," said one of the women. "It's in the little fridge next to the *tonsu*. And Eva, the plates and forks are in the cupboard next to the bookcase. I'll cut the cake. Now, who wants a foot? Who wants an ear?"

Soon the room was filled with the sound of popping champagne corks, scraping dessert forks, and female laughter.

"Attention," said another woman's voice. "There's one piece of cake left—the pièce de résistance—any takers?"

"Not me, I'm full."

"Uh-uh."

"I pass."

"No way."

"Save it for Werner—if he ever comes to."

Mr. Clarinet slipped behind the floor-length drapes that covered two walls of the room and on tiptoe, inched his way toward the light switch by the door. Laughter gave way to screams as the room went suddenly dark. In the blind confusion, Mr. Clarinet fingered the controls of the VCR. The large screen opposite the supine psychiatrist suddenly lit up. In the next five minutes, the audience viewed a replay of the scene that ensued when Clarinet and Devereux intruded on Dr. Horowitz.

Bewilderment was succeeded by curiosity as the women sat down in a semicircle on the floor facing the screen. Curiosity, in turn, was followed by outrage when they heard the psychiatrist's remark, "Seeing my twelve little creeps circle Sunshine's car . . . "

After the image of Dr. Horowitz announced, "Frankly, I would have preferred a Jewess," Mr. Devereux, still hiding behind the couch, heard a little grunting sound emanate from the live Dr. Horowitz. Then a short choking sound.

"Let's get the hell out of here," said one of the women. "We've got a plane to catch."

"Relax," said another voice. "We're only half an hour from the airport. We'll be tanning our bods on the beach in Acapulco in five hours."

Noise of boots. Sounds of laughter. Slam of door.

"Dev," said Mr. Clarinet, over the sound of the video replay, "come on out. They've gone. You won't believe what they did."

Warily, Mr. Devereux emerged from behind the couch. The two men stared down at the body of the psychiatrist. The handles of twelve silver dessert forks and a cake knife protruded from his chest. In the final analysis, the psychiatrist lay on his couch, his eyes wide open, his nostrils and mouth filled with cake.

"Oh Lord—he's dead," said Mr. Devereux, feeling in vain for a carotid pulse. He yanked one of the dessert forks from the psychiatrist's chest.

"Fawked to death. What a way to go."

"I don't think the forks did it—or this," said Mr. Clarinet, pulling the knife out of the doctor's chest. "See, the blade went in only half an inch; it didn't get through the intercostal muscles. What killed him was that piece of cake. He choked to death."

"Which piece was it?" asked Mr. Devereux.

On the screen, the late psychiatrist intoned, " . . . the penis, gentlemen, is mightier than the sword."

THE ZODIAC TOUR '76–'77

32 SUNDAY, OCTOBER 24, 1976
SCORPIO WITH VIRGO

When Dr. Sunshine walked into the examining room, the flimsily gowned woman seated on the table was inserting an ivory comb into her ebony chignon. How placid her face appeared! The sight of a seated woman, her arms raised, her hands doing something with her hair, had always impressed Dr. Sunshine—and countless sculptors of schlock garden statuary, before him—as the very quintessence of femininity. The patient's raised, slender arms pulled her full breasts up and out, enhanced the nubile flare of her pelvis and—above all—framed her lovely face. Her large, dark eyes gazed abstractedly while her hands inserted the ivory comb. She tilted her head slightly forward, exposing the downy nape of her gracile neck.

How could he tell this lovely woman that she was a man? That the nucleus in every cell of her soft, rounded body contained the XY chromosome pair of a genetic male? That she could never become pregnant because her vagina ended in a blind pouch? That in the medical sideshow behind the three-ring tent of Heart Disease, Stroke, and Cancer, she was that rarest of hormonal freaks: the man with testicular feminization?

"You're looking beautiful today, Eva—as usual."

"Thank you, Dr. Sunshine. I love your suit—is it new?"

"In a way. I bought it in London five years ago. By British standards, it's quite new."

"What did my tests show? You frightened me after my pelvic exam last week."

"I thought I told you not to worry."

"That's what frightened me."

"Eva, your tests indicate that you're a very complex woman. But I knew that the minute I first laid eyes on you."

"What do you mean?" Feeling suddenly vulnerable, she crossed her arms over her breasts. The pupils of her amethyst eyes dilated.

"First off, I must tell you that you're a healthy woman who will probably live to be 104, when you will die in the arms of your chauffeur."

"Your tests show that? I'm impressed. This chauffeur—will he be making love to me at the time or just giving me mouth-to-mouth resuscitation?"

"At that age," said Dr. Sunshine, smiling, "the distinction is academic."

"Now what do the tests really show?" asked the patient.

"They show a condition, not a disease. Eva, I'm going to give it to you straight. First of all, I'm afraid it will be impossible for you ever to get pregnant."

"Good. That fits in with my acting career nicely. But why not?"

"Quite simply, you don't have a uterus. It doesn't show up on the pelvic sonogram you had last week."

"You mean I was born without a uterus?" Her lower lip began to tremble. Dr. Sunshine squeezed her arm firmly.

"God," she said, "I knew there must be some reason I'm twenty-six and have never had a period. But I thought it was due to some hormonal imbalance. That's what my last doctor said."

"Eva, I don't have to tell you that by general appearance, you're every inch a woman. Your tests show that you're making an adequate supply of estrogen, the female hormone. But . . . "

"What?"

"You're also making, for a woman, an excessive amount of testosterone—the male sex hormone."

"But wouldn't that cause me to grow a beard and sing baritone?" She touched her smooth chin.

"Not in your case," said Dr. Sunshine. "Like any hormone, testosterone is supposed to work on every cell in the body. What's fascinating about your body, among other things, is that your cells don't react at all to testosterone. But they do react to estrogen—and that's why you're the lovely woman you are."

"I . . . I've always been attracted to men," she said. "I've always felt like a woman. Yet, there are times . . . "

"Your instincts are one hundred percent feminine!" said Dr. Sunshine, encircling her waist with his arm. As his fingertips touched her cool, smooth skin, he suddenly realized he was physically attracted to this chromosomal male born and raised with a female body. How could she know that, genetically she was a man, but was shaped like a woman, thanks to the slight but crucial dominance of her small amount of estrogen over her inactive testosterone? Dr. Sunshine decided at that moment never to tell his patient the whole truth about her genes. Life in Berkeley was complicated enough.

His reassuring pressure on her waist triggered a vermillion flush over her neck and upper chest. Twisting about, she embraced the doctor and kissed him behind his right ear.

"Did I find one of your erogenous zones?" she whispered.

"Alas, no," said Dr. Sunshine, using his W. C. Fields accent. "A map of my erogenous zones resembles the Yukon tundra—a few neglected outposts in an immense expanse of permafrost."

"Then why do I feel you getting an erection?"

"That's no erection, my dear," he said. "That's the wooden mallet I used *to whip the socks off the Duchess of Tewksberry—or Tewksbree, as she prefers to be called—in a spirited game of croquet at Withering Shanks, her lovely estate in the Cotswolds."*

"A croquet mallet?" said the patient, à la Mae West. "Well, big boy, if you've got the balls, I've got the wicket."

33 SATURDAY, MARCH 25, 1978
6:58 A.M. OAKLAND INTERNATIONAL AIRPORT

"Right this way, ladies."

Wearing an orange blazer and brown slacks, the tall, handsome Pacific Airlines booking agent gestured toward the boarding ramp of Gate 12.

Quite conditioned to taking orders from an authoritative male figure, the twelve women fell in line behind the brightly uniformed man.

"Why the V.I.P. treatment?" asked one of the women, a redhead.

"You're the only first-class passengers on this flight, and we'd like to seat you promptly."

Murmurs of approval and gratitude followed the airline official into the tunneled ramp. A smiling, Polynesian flight attendant in a sarong stood in the oval doorway at the far end.

"Aloha," she said, to no one's surprise. "Welcome aboard."

Smiling back, the twelve women followed the recorded siren song of "One Paddle, Two Paddle" into the interior of what they assumed to be a Boeing 737. Instead, it was the inside of an empty Safeway meat truck that had been backed up to the end of the boarding ramp.

Thanks to some fast footwork by the Berkeley and Oakland police, the truck had been commandeered from a nearby Safeway warehouse when the anonymous tip was phoned in that twelve suspects to two Berkeley assassinations were Acapulco-bound. The playing of a Don Ho cassette of "One Paddle, Two Paddle" on a portable tape deck had been the inspiration of Patrolman Juan Gonzales of the Oakland Police Force. He had copied the tape on his Panasonic from Oakland International's vast Muzak library.

En route by meat truck to the cooler, Officer Gonzales and three of his colleagues manacled the outraged women to one another, wrist-to-wrist, ankle-to-ankle, while Don Ho droned, "One paddle, two paddle, three pad-dle . . . "

When the last suspect was linked in the human daisy chain, Officer Gonzales said, "Girls, look at it this way: You may be up the creek, but you're not without a paddle."

"Up yours," said the redhead. "With my paddle."

THE ZODIAC TOUR '76–'77

34 TUESDAY, NOVEMBER 23, 1976 SAGITTARIUS WITH VIRGO

To Dr. Sunshine, the next best thing to lying next to a woman in bed was sitting opposite her in a restaurant. England won her great battles on the playing fields of Eton; Dr. Sunshine scored his finest conquests on the table linens of San Francisco.

A strikingly beautiful, somewhat hungry woman greatly enhanced for him the excitement of dining in a moderate-to-expensive restaurant. He and Miss Tabatha Nightingale, his British Sagittarian, were both agreeably hypoglycemic when they entered the Pier Nine Restaurant on The Embarcadero. It was a brilliant high noon as they took their seats at a center table and gazed at the azure San Francisco Bay through spectacular, floor-to-ceiling windows. Warm, heady vapors of sautéed garlic and onions emanated from the open, stainless-steel kitchen off to the right.

"A triple Tanqueray, neat, with a twist," said Dr. Sunshine to the cocktail waitress after his companion had ordered a glass of Dubonnet.

While they sipped their drinks, she said, "Before we leave here, Hillel darling, I have a little surprise for you."

"Does it involve the two of us under the table?"

"No, much more exciting than that."

A young waiter appeared—alert, charming, mustached. "Hello, I'm Stanley," he announced.

Momentarily stunned by the Tanqueray, Dr. Sunshine looked up at the waiter and asked, "Stanley, how's your sex role today?"

"Gay, as usual."

"I'm sorry—I mean your rex sole."

"Frozen, I'm afraid. Our "Fresh Catch of the Day," on the other hand, is the baked petrale, and it's wonderful."

"Really?" said Dr. Sunshine. "How lucky. I once ate at a seafood restaurant in Naples where the fresh catch of the day was a Pirelli steel-belted radial. It was floating in the bay."

"How did they serve the Pirelli?" asked Ms. Nightingale, rising to the bait.

"Al dente. And let me tell you, it was not as tough as some of the calamari I've chewed in this joint. Stanley, we'll have the cracked crab and a bottle of the Mondavi champagne."

"Very good, sir."

While the champagne was being poured, Dr. Sunshine made the mistake of peering around the room. Seated five tables away was a group of four housewives who belonged to the same PTA chapter as Mrs. Sunshine! His face blanched to the color of the napery. To all appearances, they had just sat down and not yet spotted him. Dr. Sunshine took off his aviator glasses and brought his right hand up to his face. Like a cigarette, his nose protruded between his index and third fingers.

"Darling, are you all right?"

"Waterfront restaurants tend to make me a bit seasick," he said. "Cheers!"

He downed his glass of champagne in two gulps and the waiter promptly refilled it. Dr. Sunshine prepared himself for a long, hot lunch.

Throughout the meal he managed to keep a protective hunk of crustacean or his glass of champagne in front of his face at all times. Miss Nightingale, a nonstop monologist, seized the opportunity presented by Dr. Sunshine's going into his shell, as it were, to launch into an engaging dissertation on the mystique of champagne.

"You know—don't you, Hilly?—that champagne is the drink of jockeys. The bubbles, you see, displace some of the wine, and so the tiny chaps, who are more conscious of their weight than movie stars, imbibe fewer calories per ounce. Or so they claim. Actually, your California champagnes are getting better each year, but I doubt if they'll ever surpass the great French labels. Someday you and I must hop aboard a Concorde to Paris and I'll show you . . . "

So preoccupied was he with keeping a low profile, that Dr. Sunshine was the last person in the restaurant to see it. He slowly became aware that his companion had stopped talking and was staring out the window. All around him, people were dropping forks into plates and standing up. The sunlit restaurant was abruptly plunged into deep shadow.

Dr. Sunshine looked out the window and was startled to see a gigantic aircraft carrier passing by not more than fifty yards from the waterfront. Flying a Union Jack, the behemoth made its majestic way south to its berth at Hunter's Point. Lined up at attention on deck were the two thousand officers and crew of the H.M.S. Indefatigable.

Dr. Sunshine dropped his guard for a moment and stared in awe. A hugely amplified British voice suddenly thundered into the restaurant, "AHOY, DR. SUNSHINE. MISS NIGHTINGALE LOVES YOU."

Jackknifing their arms, two thousand officers and men saluted Dr. Sunshine in perfect unison.

The doctor, for his part, raised his white napkin before his face in abject surrender as the four members of the North Berkeley PTA did an abrupt eyes-right and gasped.

Flushed with triumph and champagne, Miss Nightingale waved ecstatically at the carrier and said, "The captain is my Uncle Arthur. Splendid show, chaps!"

The waiter appeared at the table to inquire, "Can I get you anything else, sir?"

"Yes, Stanley. One torpedo, to go."

35 SATURDAY, MARCH 25, 1978
7:22 A.M. OAKLAND

When they were brought in from the airport, the twelve women were booked on 12 counts of attempted murder of Dr. Hillel Sunshine and on 144 counts of conspiracy to commit murder. When they refused to talk, they were dispatched to Highland General Hospital in Oakland for psychiatric evaluation.

Charges against them for the murder of Dr. Horowitz/Mundt were dropped for lack of sufficient evidence. (Before he and Devereux left the scene of the crime, Clarinet had fussily removed the silverware from the psychiatrist's body and wiped the murder weapon off the victim's face with party napkins. Clarinet, needless to say, was a Virgo.)

Putting on their longest faces and darkest headlines, the media prepared a shocked public for another "Trial of the Decade."

A courtroom artist who appeared to be the reincarnation of Leonardo da Vinci was introduced to an unappreciative television audience on the night of the suspects' arraignment. The artist, who signed his work, "Vince Leonard," portrayed the twelve women at a narrow table, six on either side of a thin, long-haired bailiff. The uncanny resemblance of this drawing to da Vinci's *Last Supper* was lost on the average viewer of the eleven o'clock news, but not on Vince Leonard, who knew he had sketched his masterpiece.

36 THURSDAY, MARCH 30, 1978
12:00 NOON. HERRICK HOSPITAL I.C.U.

Dr. Sunshine had never had his own medical doctor. He now had six. The neurosurgeon checked his brain and spinal cord daily. ("Oh dear, oh shit, oh dear.") The thoracic surgeon delicately adjusted his chest tubes. ("Sssss.") The vascular surgeon looked after his splenectomy wound. ("Fuuuck.")

Then came the nephrologist, who clucked over the machinations of the artificial kidney. Each morning, the pulmonary specialist twisted a few dials on the respirator, and sighed. The cardiologist galloped into the nurses' station over the lunch hour to glance at the patient's monitored EKG and to peek at the inert form of Dr. Sunshine inside his glass cubicle from across the room. That was as close as the cardiologist, a busy private practitioner, ventured, his stethoscope dangling ornamentally from his neck.

In a metal-bound chart, each of six physicians scribbled orders and progress notes that were never read by any of his five colleagues. Dr. Sunshine was in the hands of the subspecialists, a recently evolved species of physician he had regarded with extreme apprehension.

From the seclusion of his coma, Dr. Sunshine ruefully sensed the comings and goings of his six technicians. For the past five years, Dr. Sunshine had sensed that he himself was a dying breed of physician—the general internist, broadly trained to care for the entire patient. He was not vastly amused to realize that he now was a *literally* dying breed of physician. But he was still a board-certified specialist in internal medicine. From the depths of his coma, he determined to practice medicine internally as it had never been practiced before.

He would call on his steel-trap memory, which had remained completely intact. (He had always suspected a great deal of cerebration could still take place at certain levels of coma.) It was not for nothing that he had trained himself to read fifteen hundred words a minute and had religiously—Talmudically—kept himself informed of what was current in all areas of internal medicine: cardiology, pulmonary disease, nephrology, infectious disease, endocrinology, gastroenterology, rheumatology, and neurology.

Over the years, through active browsing at Berkeley's Eastern Eye bookstore, he had also acquainted himself with the major tenets of Far Eastern medicine. In deeply buried vaults of his brain, unaffected by his head injury, was encoded a vast medical library, ranging in scope from anatomy to zygogenesis, from acupuncture to Zen meditation.

Nurse Clarinet and Orderly Devereux sat in the nurses' station, gazing across the room at Dr. Sunshine stretched out in his glass cubicle.

"Look at his eyes, Dev," said Mr. Clarinet. "Always dancing up and down—he's thinking all the time. I bet he'll figure a way out. Dr. Sunshine's mind is his Ace in the hole."

"In that case," drawled Mr. Devereux, smiling broadly, "I'll be his King of Spades."

"Well, I'll be damned if I'll be his Queen of Hearts!" laughed Mr. Clarinet.

For twenty-five years, Orderly Devereux had followed with intense concentration the hospital moves of all the great Berkeley internists, including Dr. Sunshine; he had studied their chart notes and their orders, had stood with them at their patients' bedsides. Derivatively, Mr. Devereux had become one of the finest amateur internists in the West.

Unknown to the Berkeley medical community, Devereux, the son of a midwife, had been largely responsible for Herrick's excellent reputation for care of the critically ill. When he detected a major oversight, or an error of commission, by a doctor, Devereux merely instructed Clarinet to follow his own orders and not the doctor's. Knowing a good internist when he saw one, Nurse Clarinet did not hesitate to transcribe Orderly Devereux's verbal orders to the official nurses' treatment cards.

It was immediately apparent to Devereux and Clarinet that Patient Sunshine did not have a bedside internist to direct his comprehensive care. Devereux easily assumed this role, often amending and overriding the orders of the subspecialists. Thanks to the secret orders of Mr. Devereux, Dr. Sunshine received adequate nutrition through intravenous hyperalimentation, he was given quinidine every six hours to stabilize his heart rhythm, he had the precise amount of sodium and potassium added to his dialysis fluid to prevent mineral imbalance, and he received IV methicillin and gentamicin for his multiple wound infections.

For his part, Mr. Clarinet took personal charge of Dr. Sunshine's nursing care. He forbade any idle conversation at his bedside in the event the patient, though comatose, could still pick up auditory clues. With the help of a portable radio tuned to KDFC, Mr. Clarinet brought Dr. Mozart to the bedside.

He placed fresh flowers on the nightstand twice a week in hopes the patient could still smell. He instructed the female nurses to massage the patient's spastic muscles and to put all his extremities through range-of-motion exercises. He sensed the importance of keeping in touch with the comatose patient, and in this case, the importance of female touch. He strictly limited Mrs. Sunshine's daily visits to five minutes to avoid exhausting the patient, in case he could hear her, and to preserve the sanity of the nursing staff, who definitely could.

The net effect of this enlightened care was substantial. After one week, Dr. Sunshine gradually regained consciousness. Mr. Devereux succeeded in weaning him from his artificial kidney and respirator. His blood pressure, pulse rate, and temperature returned to normal.

But despite this progress, Dr. Sunshine still lay silent and motionless in bed.

After his first ten days in the glass cubicle on the Intensive Care Unit, his neurosurgeon made the melancholy diagnosis of "Locked-in Syndrome"—a brain stem disorder characterized by language comprehension, ability to breathe, ability to open and close one's eyes, ability to look up and down—but inability to do anything else. Dr. Sunshine could not move, speak, or eat. He could feel neither touch, nor pain, nor pressure.

He was locked-in.

37 SUNDAY, APRIL 16, 1978
9:00 A.M. HERRICK HOSPITAL I.C.U.

"Hilly. It's Gloria. I'm back, honey. My poor baby. You look awful! Do you hurt? I asked the doctors if they were giving you pain medicine, but they said you don't need it. That you can't feel anything. So I asked, 'How in hell do you know?' They say you have something—that you're locked-in, they call it—that you can hear and see and breathe and stuff, but you can't move or speak. Oh Hilly, how awful! So I said to the nurse, 'If he can hear, maybe he can feel. You don't really know. Maybe he hurts like hell under all those bandages and he can't tell us!' Oh God, Hilly, I'm sorry. I know I shouldn't cry. You're the one going through the meat grinder. I just *know* you're in pain. So finally I had to go yell at Clarinet, and now he's paging the neurosurgeon. I know Dr. Edwards will give you something for the pain. My poor Hilly! You're so bunged up! How can this have happened? Why would a bunch of crazy women attack your car? The police think maybe they belonged to a feminist cult. I could kill them! It's all over the papers. Anyhow, the cops are still grilling them and they're not talking. Oh Hilly, why did I ever let you con me into leaving Pittsburgh? I told you Berkeley was full of crazies. You fell in love with that stupid view and dragged me out here to Berserkeley and now a bunch of weirdos have killed you. Oh my sweet love! I didn't mean that. You're not going to die, my darling. You can't! I need you so much. What? Oh, it's you, Mr. Clarinet. When did you come in? Time's up already? But I just got here! All right, all right. I'm leaving. But don't worry, Hilly. I'm going to speak to Dr. Edwards about getting you some morphine. I won't let you down, darling. I'm going to stay right by your side and help you and talk to you as long as you live!"

THE ZODIAC TOUR '76–'77

38 WEDNESDAY, DECEMBER 22, 1976 CAPRICORN WITH VIRGO

With tremulous fingertips, he inched up the sheer face of her inner thigh, seeking . . .

"What's that?" she asked.

"What's what?"

"That bump?"

"What beump?" he asked, in a highly distracted effort to imitate Inspector Clouseau.

"Right where you're touching. Is it a wart, or what?"

"Cassie, I can't see," he said, sitting up and reaching for his glasses. She snapped on the bedside lamp.

"Oh that," he said, inspecting the three-millimeter blot on the Capricorn's escutcheon. "That's just a seborrheic keratosis. Completely benign. I've got two on my wrist just like it."

"Oh yeah, you sure do," she said, squinting at Dr. Sunshine's wrist. "Thank you." She turned off the light.

"Don't mention it," he said. He removed his glasses in the dark and set off from her bump for warmer regions.

"I once had a boyfriend who had herpes," she announced.

Dr. Sunshine lunged for the light switch and his glasses.

"Don't worry, Hilly. I never let him come near me after he told me."

"I hope not," he said.

"You know, I get these funny little pains below my left breast," she said. "What do you think causes them?"

"You mean here?" he asked, groping in the dark.

"Yeah. Ouch—you're pressing too hard!"

"Sorry. That's nothing but a sore rib. You've got a touch of costochondritis. Probably from working out in the gym."

"You're very nice," she said, wrapping her arms around his neck and kissing him.

"Ouch!" he said. "You're pinching a nerve in my neck."

"I'm sorry, Hilly. . . . Speaking of necks, mine sometimes makes a sound like Rice Krispies when I turn my head."

"Oh, that's just a little grating of facets—nothing to it."

"How come both my big toes are numb?" she asked, massaging his neck lightly.

"It's those Japanese sandals you wear."

"You mean my zories?"

"Yes. The strap that goes between your first and second toes can cause local numbness."

"Gee, how did you figure that out?"

"Ever since my first attack of gout, I've become a student of the big toe. Let me ask you something, Cassie. As a little girl, did you and your boyfriend sometimes play Doctor?"

"No, mine was such a dreary childhood; I remember playing Social Worker once with my brother. Why do you ask?"

"For one thing, our foreplay has consisted of a most stimulating recitation of our symptoms."

"Yeah, I know. When you mentioned that pinched nerve in your neck, I got this deep, throbbing sensation in my pelvis."

Dr. Sunshine sat up in bed, turned on the lamp, and said, "Congratulations, Cassie. On our very first effort at lovemaking, we've managed to achieve mutual sarcasm."

She stared at the doctor sternly for a moment, then collapsed in laughter across his lap. Catlike, Poindexter sprang awake and stretched—then, to Dr. Sunshine's horror, went limp. The deadly exchange of physical symptoms had turned Poindexter off.

"I've got a new symptom for you," said Dr. Sunshine. "Impotence."

Over the next half hour, despite all their efforts, which included petting, cajoling, and strangulation, Poindexter refused to budge.

"You dumb schmuck!" shouted Dr. Sunshine to Poindexter, who pretended not to hear.

Suddenly, tears started from his Capricorn's eyes.

"Oh, Hilly," she said, "I don't care—I still love you."

Her tremulous voice touched a responsive chord in Poindexter.

"Look!" said Dr. Sunshine, gesturing proudly at his sidekick.

"Wow," she said, her eyes riveted. "Now I know how Jack felt at his first sight of the bean stalk."

"Jack be nimble, Jack be quick," urged Dr. Sunshine.

"But that's Jack of the candlestick, not the bean stalk," she said.

"I'm in no mood to discuss comparative anatomy," said Dr. Sunshine. "Let's hurry up and play Jack-in-the-Box before old Jack Frost sets in."

Poindexter, that jack of one trade, put an end to this badinage by doing his amusing impersonation of a jackhammer.

❂ ❂ ❂

Two nights later, his Capricorn insisted that Dr. Sunshine attend Christmas Eve mass with her at an Episcopalian church in the Oakland hills. When he refused, she broke down and said he didn't love her. Actually, he didn't love her, but he also didn't want to lose her. Lust, he conceded, imposed its obligations, too. After much soul-searching, he agreed to go to mass.

Dr. Sunshine calculated that the church's congregation was so far removed geographically, spiritually, and politically from the People's Republic of Berkeley, that it was unlikely that any of his patients would be in attendance. Secondly, he convinced himself that a one-hour exposure to an Episcopalian mass would more likely lead to the diversion, rather than the conversion, of this Jew.

The first half hour in church passed without incident. He almost permitted himself to relax. What he had not counted on was the obligatory procession of the entire congregation to the altar to partake of the wafer and the wine.

While those around him rose as one, he adamantly remained seated with his legs crossed and his arms folded across his chest. Standing above him, his lovely companion shot him a most menacing, blue-eyed look. He felt himself gradually rising to his feet.

They were halfway down the crowded aisle leading to the altar, when he saw inching toward him none other than his distinguished colleague, Dr. Barry Shapiro, and his shiksa! The young cardiologist's lips were empurpled with wine; a sprinkling of wafer crumbs flecked the lapels of his navy blue jacket. *The two doctors exchanged bland, unseeing glances in a futile effort to will into reality the fact that Drs. Sunshine and Shapiro could not possibly be attending mass at the Second Episcopalian Church of Oakland.*

Dr. Sunshine abruptly wanted out. Just before reaching the altar, he slipped his right hand under his jacket and activated his beeper. "Whoops!" *he said, turning off the piercing sound.* "Sorry, sweetie, I've got to get to a phone." *He turned and shoved his way toward the exit through a living wall of pink, pleasantly scented Episcopalians.*

She followed him closely, shouting, "You can't fool me! I saw you reach for your pants and fiddle with your thingee before it went off!"

Dr. Sunshine turned and said, "I wouldn't think of doing that in church. Why, it would be a shonda for de goyim."*

---

39 MONDAY, APRIL 17, 1978
5:30 A.M. HERRICK HOSPITAL I.C.U.

"Bockwurst. My arms and legs—paralyzed—dead-white links of bockwurst. Thin-skinned veal sausages—pale, cold, numb. I can't feel a thing. But I can hear. I can see. I can move my eyes, but only up and down.

"Jesus, I'm locked-in.

"I have a perpetual erection—not much feeling there, either. Good old Poindexter! Stout fellow! *Brat*wurst! Rising above my dead body, giving The Finger to the world!

"Thank God I can think. But I can't move, I can't speak! I'm locked-in! This must be what it's like to be in hell. I can't say a word and Gloria won't stop talking.

"They've got me strapped to this Stryker frame so they can turn me like a male chauvinist pig on a spit.

"I'm not hungry. Terrific. I'll lose a few pounds—*The Berkeley 30-Day Coma Diet.*

"God, I can't feel anything or anyone. I can't even wiggle my toes. Somebody once said, 'Since death is very still, keep moving.'

---

*an embarrassment in front of the gentiles

"ALL POINTS BULLETIN TO ALL VIABLE
CELLS AND INTRACELLULAR ORGANELLES:
KEEP MOVING, MOTHERFUCKERS!"

"Locked-in. So this is my reward for thinking I could circumforni-cate the zodiac—make love in one year with every sign under the sun. God, forgive me. My only celestial inspiration and I blew it. Another Icarus, flying too close to the sun—right, God? Right, Zeus?

"I hope you're listening, God. Please—I have no one else to talk to, no one to confess to. If these were Biblical times, I'd beg you to be my shepherd. If this were World War II, I'd sign you on as my co-pilot. Now, in 1978, I'm appointing you my psychiatrist—someone who gives the impression of listening. God, let me try to explain how I screwed up my life.

"Part of my trouble, God, was Berkeley—that Hanging Garden of Babble-on, that Western outpost of elitism. And eroticism. To be part of the Berkeley establishment, it wasn't sufficient for a doctor merely to practice medicine. Oh, no. He or she had to excel in at least one other field. Milton Rappaport, the pediatrician, was into middle-game chess theory. Al Nachman, the gynecologist, was into world hunger. Steve Korngold, the proctologist, was into Kirlian photog-raphy. Hilly Sunshine, the internist, was into women.

"If only Sid Cohn had not died so young, I wouldn't be lying here. Cohn, Berkeley's premier internist and my idol, dead at forty-seven, when I was thirty-five. Cohn, the self-proclaimed Elemental Man, be-cause the letters of his last name were symbols of the four elements essential to life: carbon, oxygen, hydrogen, nitrogen—as if I needed to remind you, Old Man.

"Sid knew exactly what hit him—a massive infarct, the sudden blanching of sixty percent of his heart muscle. Dead-right diagnosti-cian to the end.

"A tiny plug of fat and clotted blood—the size of a match head—closed off his left main coronary and stopped all that knowledge, that compassion, that great laugh, that good marriage.

"Before they scattered his ashes—carbon—over the Pacific, the family placed them in a beautiful wooden box. On the lid was painted an oak tree in full autumnal blaze. The box rested on the family's Steinway in the music room of their Maybeck house on Cragmont.

"Sid's daughter and three sons tearfully played Beethoven's last quartets at twilight for those of us who jammed the Cohn household the day after he died. As I sat there—Gloria was home with the kids—I could sense a number of Sid's patients sizing me up as their next internist. (And what young internist will they size up at *my* memorial?)

"Suddenly, my beeper went off and the Fourteenth Quartet became a quintet until I could shut the damn thing off.

"I called my answering service from the upstairs master bedroom. A fifty-two-year-old widowed patient of mine had sprained her back and couldn't get out of bed. With profuse apologies, she asked if I would make a house call. I stared at the smooth, cool surface of the Cohns' conjugal bed and hung up.

"Did I make a house call! Was my patient grateful! Did she look terrific! Did I find a way to throw back in her thrown-out back! Was Louise a celebration of life after a lament for the dead!"

40 WEDNESDAY, APRIL 19, 1978
3:00 A.M. HERRICK HOSPITAL I.C.U.

"Oh God, after fourteen years, the virginity of a faithful marriage was lost to a fifty-two-year-old widow with a sprained back. Louise! An elegant, beautiful widow, who thanked me and thanked You, and awakened in Poindexter a long-dormant lust—a lust I hadn't felt since the early years of my marriage.

"Oh God, I had always found temptation irresistible. Until Louise sprained her back, I had somehow contrived to discourage its appearance. Gloria was the first woman I had made love to; fourteen years later, Louise was the second.

"Louise knew I treasured my family and my practice. After three months, she left on a solitary cruise around the world to keep me from destroying all I cared for, including her. I missed her terribly. To help me recover from losing her, I began seeing other women. What began as a one-shot antidote to death soon became an addiction—with

Poindexter serving as my pusher. To help me recover from the other women, I began seeing Sam Horowitz, the psychiatrist.

"He urged me to court Gloria again, but by this time I was too addicted to shiksas to make more than a halfhearted try. What is this fatal attraction of Jewish guys to blondes? You'd think after reading Philip Roth and Arthur Miller, I'd have gladly taken up hang gliding.

"After a year, Dr. Horowitz was able to classify me as having 'a narcissistic character disorder tinged with sociopathic tendencies,' thus successfully completing my therapy. Now that I had insight, I was comforted to know that I wasn't so much cheating on my wife as merely *acting out*.

"After two more years of acting out, a shiksa whom I'd jilted blew the whistle on me. More precisely, she mailed Gloria a packet of my love notes, erotically illustrated in my inimitable hand.

"With this woman, I had met my first femme fatale. And she was a beaut!

"Erroll Flynn once observed that his love affairs lasted for the brief interval between the time when his paramour looked like a goddess and when she began to resemble a haddock. One night, as I chanced upon a faint gill slit while nuzzling my first femme fatale behind her ear, she announced that we were destined never to part. Our eternal bond, she insisted, was based on the fortuitous conjunction of our ruling planets. I tried to convince her that it was the premeditated conjunction of our less than heavenly bodies that inspired her conclusion. But she was unyielding.

"In the end, I announced as tactfully as possible that I could no longer continue to see her. She glared at me for a few moments and then rather tenderly, I thought, kissed me goodnight. The next afternoon, my wife received the special delivery parcel with seventeen cents postage (and a pound of my flesh) due.

"For the next two months, Gloria didn't speak to me. She herself consulted my friend the psychiatrist, slimmed down to her premarital weight of 114 pounds, began taking guitar lessons, and got a job in San Francisco managing an art gallery.

"Good old Sam Horowitz helped Gloria recover her sanity. What a wily shrink! He agreed with her that I was a schmuck, but not a bad father or provider. He encouraged her to assert her beauty and her independence by losing weight and getting a job. Sam knew how to patch up my damaged women. He rehabilitated my wife. I fucked his.

"One morning, just before she left for work, Gloria placed a grenade in my egg cup by announcing that she had recently concluded a satisfactory affair with a divorce lawyer in San Francisco. After picking up my pieces from every cranny in our breakfast nook, I called Sam Horowitz, and accused him of overachieving. Sam insisted the affair was Gloria's idea, not his. In fact, he said, he strongly recommended against it.

"Oh, God, I was demolished—crushed under the dumbbell weight of the Double Standard. I took a leave of absence from my office and my senses and spent five sleepless days and nights in bed. On the sixth day, first Poindexter, then I, rose from the bed. I stormed out of the house and spent a week exhausting the oil reserves of Berkeley's darkest massage parlors.

"When I finally consented to meet Gloria on neutral territory— Trader Vic's Tiki Room in San Francisco—she proposed terms for a cessation of hostilities. She would agree to resume our marriage on one condition: either we both took lovers or we both didn't. Since it had been my observation that open-ended marriages were usually dead in the center, I suggested that we both lay off.

"Gloria grabbed my hand and said that if she ever found out that I was having another affair, she would take the children and disappear. We spent the rest of our lunch crying into our Bongo-Bongo soup."

41 THURSDAY, APRIL 20, 1978 4:00 A.M. HERRICK HOSPITAL I.C.U.

"Our marriage had seemed like such a good idea, once upon a time. Until we married, we each had spent half our lives fighting off people who lusted after us and the other half lusting after people who fought *us* off. After marriage, our mutual lust evolved into mutual trust, which accrued at an annual rate of about six percent. And then came the trust-busters: the merry widow and the jilted shiksa.

"When I found out, shortly after our Tiki Room Accord, that Gloria still didn't trust me, I was outraged. After being followed for three days to and from my office by a fair, blue-eyed woman in a red TR-3, it dawned on me that she was a private eye. Well, if *that* was the game Gloria was playing, I vowed from then on it would be an eye for an eye.

"I hired my own detective, who proved to be as inept as my wife's was vulnerable. He charged me six hundred dollars for a set of twelve underexposed, Polaroid snapshots of Gloria having lunch at Chez Panisse with her father!

"Meanwhile, her private eye, the goddess in the TR-3, had electronically bugged my office. She spent two days in earphones listening to me treat my patients. The detective was so taken with my impeccably professional conduct, that she accosted me in my office garage one night after work, threw her arms around my neck, and sobbed, 'I've been looking for a doctor like you for years! I've got these headaches you won't believe!'

"She resigned from my wife's case—and I accepted hers—on the spot. We repaired to a headache clinic on Oakland's motel row where her symptoms temporarily abated and my adultery permanently relapsed. Oh, God.

"Gloria's job in the city made my resumption of womanizing virtually fail-safe. My love for shiksas had proved as imperishable as plastic. I was soon panting over a blonde who had headaches and a TR-3. God, what did Gloria do wrong—besides marrying me—to deserve me?

"After the private eye, I went public. Spurred on by Poindexter, I found myself sometimes making love to two, and once, three women a day: morning (a redhead), noon (a blonde), and night (a brunette). I became a color-coordinated lady-killer—a regular Bluebeard of Happiness.

"Oh God, how can any long-term marriage, no matter how stable, compete in glamour and excitement with an affair? I wrestled with that question for years. Of course, You needn't guess *how* I wrestled, or with whom.

"Berkeley in the sixties had been a hotbed of sexual freedom. In the seventies, the bed was still warm. Following Poindexter, I jumped right in and pulled the covers over my head."

42 SATURDAY, APRIL 22, 1978
10:00 A.M. HERRICK HOSPITAL I.C.U.

"Hello, my darling. I'm back. Can you feel it when I kiss you? I still can't believe that you can't. Dr. Edwards absolutely assures me that you aren't hurting. He used lots of Latin words to convince me. Oh God, Hilly, I hope he's right. He says if they gave you morphine it might kill you, because your breathing is already so depressed. Oh, Hilly, sometimes I wonder if that would be best. You must be so horribly bored and depressed, stuck in there and hurting. Are you frightened, my love? They say only one in a thousand people ever get out once they're locked-in, but I know you'll do it. And then you'll come home to us. I've got good news, darling—you don't have to worry about your practice. Sol Feldman's group has been seeing all your patients and he says they're doing just fine. Sol says there have been absolutely no complaints, and he and his partners will be happy to keep seeing them as long as necessary. And I checked about your disability insurance—thank God I made you take it out! You won't believe this, Hilly, but you'll be making more money from your disability than you did from your practice! Isn't that marvelous! The kids are worried about you, sweetheart, of course, but I keep telling them to be brave and Daddy will come home soon. It's going to be better when you come home, Hilly, I promise. I won't get so mad anymore about little things. I won't keep working you over about that shiksa who sent me those illustrated love letters. I know she didn't mean anything to you, and I know how sorry you are. Anyhow that was so long ago. Time to forget about her—I promise to try. I feel guilty, you know, because I've never really trusted you again, but I will now. This last year has been pretty good, hasn't it, my love? You've been home a lot, we've been doing more family stuff, and fixing up the house, and then at night, wow, it's like Venice again! Oh Hilly, you can't die!

Don't leave me. Honey, I don't want to embarrass you, but I have to tell you—every time I come to visit, you get an erection. It's true. There he stands—Mr. Zucchini. Ram-packed the whole time I'm here. Can you feel me, Hilly? I'm stroking Mr. Zucchini. It just can't be possible that he doesn't feel anything. Sweet, sweet, Mr. Zucchini . . . Listen Hilly, you know how psychic I am. Let's try it now. I'll keep stroking Mr. Zucchini, and I'll get real quiet, and you can send me your thoughts. Okay. Slow, and sweet, and still. Just send 'em out, baby, and I'll catch 'em . . . I think I can feel your mind reaching out. That's right . . . Oh yes, Hilly, yes. I love you, too . . . I know you're sorry, my darling. I forgive you. I really do. I know you'd never do it again . . . You really mean that, Hilly? You love how I move? Oh, Hilly! But then why did you . . . ? Oh God, let's don't go into that again. Tell me more . . . No, you're right—it's true. You can't ever make it up to me, but yes, my darling, you may try. Hilly, now I'm getting hot, too. Maybe I could . . . No, dammit, the door to this glass box doesn't lock. I was thinking I could pull the curtains around the bed and climb on top. . . .

"Goddamit, Clarinet, haven't you ever heard of knocking? What's wrong with this place? It's not possible to have any privacy here! If you ring for a nurse you can wait six years, but if you want a little privacy, in they walk. Hilly, I'll be back in a little while. I'm going down to the police station. Apparently they've finally gotten a confession from those maniacs who tried to kill you, and the prosecutors want to talk to me before it gets in the papers. Then I'll come back my love, and we can take up where we left off."

THE ZODIAC TOUR '76–'77

43 FRIDAY, JANUARY 21, 1977 AQUARIUS WITH VIRGO

It was one of Dr. Sunshine's ambitions to write, in his declining years, a biography of Poindexter entitled Phallus in Wonderland. *One chapter, as he envisioned it, would begin:*

"Of all the misadventures of Poindexter, impo

t

e

n

c

e was perhaps the most

tragic and premature ejac!ulation, the most comic."

It was at the outset of Dr. Sunshine's affair with Maggie Weems, a forty-ish flower girl, that premature ejac!ulation struck. She was an ethereal, blue-eyed beauty with a diamond in her nose. Maggie had been his patient in the early sixties when she left to "follow her bliss." And now, fourteen years later, she had returned from Tibet to Berkeley. As they hugged in his office, their compressed bodies released a comingled scent of Lagerfeld cologne and patchouli oil.

Her classic 1962 Levi's, after more than a decade of wash-and-wear, had achieved the texture of Benares silk and the pallor of poinsettia leaves grown in a cave. Her heirloom tee shirt bore the faded legend, "Flower Power."

"It's so good to see you again, Hilly," she said. "You look fabulous."

"Beauty is in the nose—I mean the eye—of the beholder," he said, blushing. "What brings you down from the Himalayas, Maggie?"

"Disenchantment. After fourteen years of waiting on my guru hand and foot, I never once achieved enlightenment—but he finally did. One night last month, while I was washing his feet, he overturned the basin, grabbed me, and said he loved me."

"What a martyr to have waited so long! How did you react?"

"Well, after fourteen years, I had grown accustomed to his feet. But his face was another matter. I figured if I wanted a bearded little wacko chasing after me, I might as well come back to Berkeley and have my choice."

"It must be quite a culture shock for a sixties flower girl to return to Berkeley in the uptight seventies."

"It is. I miss the bracing smell of Mace in the air, the tinkle of broken shop windows. Most of all, of course, I miss being young. Let's face it, you're looking at the last rose of the Summer of Love."

"You still look great," said Dr. Sunshine. "Listen, we've all done time, Maggie."

"Yes, but look at you! It isn't fair. We're both forty-one years old and you haven't aged a bit except for a little gray at the temples."

"There's a lot more than meets the eye," said Dr. Sunshine. "Thanks to a certain formula, you're looking at Grecian temples."

Having been monogamous in the sixties, he surprised her by suggesting they meet at her apartment in North Berkeley. Her eyes blinked, her diamond winked, and she accepted. The pursuit of her bliss had led her back to Dr. Sunshine. No more bearded little wackos for her! (Rather, a clean-shaven tall one—as she later found out.)

When she greeted him at her front door on Benvenue Avenue, he found her wearing only her diamond, a trace of Shalimar perfume, a pale blue scarf of Benares silk around her neck, and ankle bells. All those years in the frozen Himalayas had preserved her magnificent figure. They exchanged a feverish hug and a lingering kiss. Poindexter was beside himself. Dr. Sunshine abruptly broke off the kiss.

"What's the matter?" she asked.

"Your, uh, diamond. It's scratching my glasses."

After he slowly undressed, they repaired to her shogun-sized futon. The setting sun glanced off brass trays, ivory elephants, gold-embossed incense boxes, and the diamond in her nose. India's third-best sitar player produced a sinuous whine that uncoiled cobralike from her hi-fi set, while Fumes of Exhilaration, India's 78th-best incense, burned in the capacious navel of a supine, pewter monkey.

As they embraced again, Dr. Sunshine groaned.

"What's the matter?" she asked, rising up on one elbow and stroking his hairy chest with her ringed fingers.

"Nothing," he said, squirming a foot away from her. "I'm too excited— your perfume, your body, that rock in your nose—just don't touch me for a minute."

"Oh, I get it. You're about to have a premature—"

"Don't say it! Just let me cool down for a few seconds, okay?"

"But, baby, I can help you. Haven't you heard of Masters and Johnson's squeeze technique?"

Both Dr. Sunshine and Poindexter blenched.

"Yes, I have," said the doctor, *"and speaking for Poindexter, I choose not to be squeezed."*

"Oh don't be absurd, Hilly. There's nothing to it. Here . . . "

With a jangle of ankle bells, she pounced on Poindexter and clamped his turgid forehead in the vise of her long-nailed thumbs and index fingers.

Speaking again for Poindexter, Dr. Sunshine emitted a shriek. In a frenzy of pain, he wrestled Poindexter from her pincers maneuver and doubled up, moaning.

"Are you all right?" she asked.

"I'm O.K.," he said. *"But Poindexter here will never be the same. You've crushed his brain—which is just as well. He's been masterminding my downfall ever since I first laid hands on him."*

"But your, ah, premature ejaculation—how's that coming along?"

"Fine, fine. Now what do you suggest for my premature emasculation?"

"Let me show you," she said.

"Okay, but this time, don't use your fingernails."

She writhed toward him, faintly jingling her ankle bells, subtly distilling an essence of Shalimar. The face she had turned in ecstasy five thousand times toward Himalayan sunsets, she turned toward him.

Thanks to giving Masters and Johnson's squeeze technique another chance, he made the Aquarian's ankle bells ring for an hour and twenty minutes.

44 SUNDAY, APRIL 23, 1978
5:10 A.M. HERRICK HOSPITAL I.C.U.

"Dear God, between the solidarity of my family life and the demands of Poindexter—that is, between a rock and a hard place—my sanity finally began breaking up in 1975. Funny thing—while I was losing my mind, I'd never looked better in my life. The aerobics of womanizing had done wonders for my physical health.

"Philandering turned this romancer into a necromancer—a sexual magician with his slightly bent magic wand. For Poindexter and me, the Houdini-like need for precise timing, perfect deception, and consistently peak performance had transformed the joy of sex into a frenzied vaudeville act of one-night stands.

"I became an exhausted sorcerer with a burned-out apprentice. In the end, I longed to recreate that most difficult of illusions— monogamy. That's when I conjured up my cosmic Twelve-Step program. With the assistance of a digital computer—that most contemporary means of prestidigitation—I finally achieved monogamy through astrology, that most ancient form of hocus-pocus.

"To my astonishment, almost all the women who were attracted to me read their horoscopes daily. And each of them had a college degree! Can you explain that, God?

"I must say, all of them pegged me as a Virgo on first sight.

"As far as I was concerned, astrology explained the human condition as irrationally as any other organized system of beliefs. To tell the truth, the geocentricity—the central role of Earth—implicit in astrology, appealed to me. As a member of the orthodox scientific community, I had never been overjoyed with a cosmos that was indifferent to the existence of Hillel Isaiah Sunshine.

"In a word, astrology's geocentricity complemented my egocentricity. Don't laugh. I'm not nearly the narcissist You are. A lot of people say You created man in Your own image. For all I know, You're the spitting image of Carl Sagan.

"I'm only a minor narcissist. I never thought I was God's gift to women, but, rather, women were merely God's gift to me. Thanks anyway, Old Man."

45 THURSDAY, JUNE 15, 1978
9:15 A.M. HERRICK HOSPITAL I.C.U.

From his hospital bed, Dr. Sunshine agonized over the memory of the twelve zodiac women. He had a clear image of each of them, first as lovers, then as killers. What could have possessed them? Why would they want to kill him? He had been so certain Sam Horowitz had calmed them all down.

Oh, he could understand why they might still be miffed at him. He had, after all, systematically dumped each of them once the sun had fled her sector of the zodiac. They all appeared so *stunned* when he left them. A thirty-one-night stand, he had to admit, was a cruel limit to set on a promising affair—it was the sexual equivalent of an orchestra storming out of the hall after playing the first movement of the *Jupiter* Symphony.

But he had taken such pains to protect the women from a letdown! Had emphatically warned them not to fall in love with him! Had given each of them at least forty-eight hours' notice! Had lavished gifts on them—zodiac pendants from Tiffany's for god's sake! Had truly adored them! Had flattered them! Had amused them! What did women *want*?

Often, it turned out, they didn't want him. But so many did, that Dr. Sunshine shrugged off the not infrequent resistance to his subtle advances.

After saying good-by to the last of his Sun Signs—a Pisces—and packing her off to Dr. Horowitz, he enjoyed a year of blissful monogamy during which, from time to time, he thought of his dozen damsels, always with the most tender of sentiments. Then, the explosion on Oxford Street. And now, a destroyed body, a damaged brain, a million-to-one chance for survival.

What had he done to deserve this?

THE ZODIAC TOUR '76–'77

46 MONDAY, FEBRUARY 21, 1977
PISCES WITH VIRGO

There was something about her eyes. A fleeting, greenish gold glint at the edge of each blue iris. But he would get to her eyes later. For the time being he addressed himself to the chief complaint of this water-clear blonde—her tremor.

As she sat on the examining table, the tremor was evident only to the trained eye. But when Dr. Sunshine asked her to undress, her fingers danced chaotically over her buttons and zippers. He had to assist her in removing her bra. And now as she sat nude before him, he asked her to hold her arms out in front of herself. She winced in embarrassment as her delicate hands flapped like birds' wings at the ends of her slender, perfectly tapered arms.

"Does anyone in your family shake like this?" asked the doctor.

"I don't know—I was raised by foster parents."

She rested her hands in her lap, and in that soft downy nest, the wing-beat quieted down. Dr. Sunshine gave her shoulder a paternal pat. Instinctively, she shrugged away. The doctor cleared his throat and resumed his quest for a diagnosis.

"The liver function tests were slightly abnormal—nothing to write home about," he said. "Sara, did you ever have hepatitis?"

"Yes—my second year in high school. Yellow eyeballs—the whole bit."

"You aren't a heavy drinker, are you?"

"I'm a frequent drinker—I go out a lot—but not a heavy one."

Dr. Sunshine proceeded with his neurologic exam. Her knee jerks were normal. She did not have Babinski toe signs. Reaching into his pocket, he said, "I'd like you to close your eyes while I put a familiar object in your right hand. Feel it and tell me what it is."

He placed a coin in her right hand. Her tremor increased as she ran her fingers over it.

"It's a penny," she said, and the coin dropped to the floor. "Oh, I'm sorry."

"Don't be," said Dr. Sunshine, stooping to retrieve it. When he stood up, he stared at Lincoln's shiny profile and turned pale with excitement. He had just reached down for a copper penny and come up with diagnostic gold. As he removed the wall-mounted ophthalmoscope, his hands were shaking almost as much as hers.

He trained the thin beam of light from the instrument onto her blue iris with its greenish gold rim. There was something about her eyes, all right— Kayser-Fleischer rings: speckled bands of copper deposits about the iris seen in only one disease in medicine.

When he snapped the room light back on, she said, "A penny for your thoughts, Doctor. You look like you've just seen a ghost."

"I have. The ghost of Dr. Samuel Wilson, the man who first described what's ailing you. Listen to me—you're going to be okay. But if I had blown the diagnosis of Wilson's disease, his ghost—and yours—would have haunted me the rest of my days."

"What's Wilson's disease?"

"It's a form of copper toxicity. From both your biologic parents, you inherited a tendency to absorb an excessive amount of copper from your diet. Your liver, part of your brain, and the rims of your blue eyes are all copper-

plated—for the time being. Goddam—Wilson's disease, and it's only Monday!"

"I wish I could share your enthusiasm, Dr. Sunshine. How can you get all that copper out?"

"It's not going to be easy. You've got to take a copper-binding drug called pencillamine the rest of your life. Now for the good news—the effects are often spectacular. I can almost promise you that your tremor will eventually disappear, and your liver function will greatly improve."

Tears shone in her eyes.

"Dr. Sunshine, I didn't want to tell you this before—but you're the fifth doctor I've gone to for help. The others all told me my tremor was due to my nerves and my abnormal liver tests were from my old bout of hepatitis."

"Too bad. They didn't have my lucky penny."

"Now that I'm a walking copper mine, Doctor," she said, touching his shoulder, "would you like to sink a shaft?"

"Are you trying to contribute to the delinquency of a 'miner'?"

✦ ✦ ✦

Her skin! In his decades of unpublished research on womankind, he had never seen, felt, inhaled skin like hers. Hers was restive skin—skin that paled, blushed, warmed, cooled, moistened, in response to the subtlest of stimuli. Was it the excess of copper in her epidermis that gave her skin its luster, its electricity?

"Who knows? Who cares?" thought Dr. Sunshine, as they undressed in the plant-filled bedroom of her cedar A-frame high in the Berkeley hills. Satin sheets of pale champagne on a hand-rubbed walnut bed invited the imprint of their bodies.

Their first embrace created so much static charge that her sheets clung to their backs like skin grafts. It did not take Dr. Sunshine long to discover that his perfect blonde was copper-wired for multiple orgasms. With trembling hands, he gently parted her thighs. . . .

To understand the origins of a California earthquake, one must go back three billion years, when a cold slab of lithosphere was thrust down through the tender skin of Mother Earth into the warm mantle of her interior. One must then imagine a cataclysmic coming together of two adjacent tectonic plates, followed by an increase in heat, a sudden liquefaction, a rising blob of magma, and then a tremor. A tremor ascending from a focal point deep within, until it breaks the surface in a pulsatile wave that spends itself in a convulsion. A convulsion, which one observer has likened to that of a terrier shaking a rat.

When the earthquake of February 21, 1977, struck the cedar and glass house, Dr. Sunshine and his Pisces were in the midst of an eruption of their own creation. The initial impact of the quake shoved the bed out from under them. Shaking variously with lust, fear, and Wilson's disease, they rode out the first wave of the temblor on the bedroom carpet. After an eternity of seconds, the room stopped its horrific shaking. They found themselves covered with the leaves of exotic plants that had crashed down from ceiling hooks. Her copper-rimmed, electric-blue eyes stared up at him through the foliage of a Saxifraga sarmentosa.

"Oh Hilly, did you—"

"Don't say it."

"—feel the earth move?"

"You said it."

"Oh God, Hilly, I've always loved sex, but it's never been like this. You're the first man I've ever gone to bed with who's come up with special effects."

"How much do you think it measured?"

"Nine inches, at least."

"Don't give Poindexter a swelled head. I was referring to the Richter scale."

"Oh, I'd give it a seven point two."

"Sounds about right."

Still within her, he felt the after-throbs of her latest orgasm, while without, the aftershocks of the quake gently rocked the house.

47 FRIDAY, JUNE 16, 1978
8:15 A.M. HERRICK HOSPITAL I.C.U.

"You bastard! You slimy son-of-a-bitch! They say you can see. Can you see that, Hilly, you shiksa-sucking shithead? No, Devereux, I am not trying to smother him with the newspaper. I'm showing him the headlines. You stay the fuck out of this. Can you read it, my pig-shit swine of an ex-husband? All about your Twelve Avenging Furies? Only they got it wrong, my lately beloved, because Number Thirteen is right here! Your lucky number! You fucked one a month for a year? Last year? You cynical, conniving cocksucker! God, how I hate you! You did all this after you promised me you never would again? Besides the first shiksa, and now these twelve, how many more were there, you scheming low-lying ratfucker! The only good thing about living in Berkeley, it's given me the vocabulary to tell you what I think of you. You asshole! How could you? Goddamit, Hilly, why did you do this to me? My mother warned me never to trust you again, but oh, no, I believed *you*! The phone's been ringing and ringing—everybody in town feels sorry for me. To hear my friends tell it, I'm the only person on the planet who ever believed in you! People have started bringing me casseroles! I feel like such a fucking fool. God*damn* you! And there you lie with your fucking erection! Except the stupid thing's not even straight up—it tips off to the right, did you know that, Hilly? You can take Mr. Zucchini and shove it! SHUT UP, Devereux! He's still my husband, until the divorce papers are final. I can yell at him if I want! I may just stand here and yell at him for the next ten years. You bastard. You lying, cheating . . . Call the police then. I don't care. I'm *not* going to hurt him. I could do it, you know, Hilly. I really could kill you. Sneak in here at night and finish you off. It would be easy. Or at least cut off your goddamned cock, your leaning tower of zucchini! No jury would convict me—they'd call it justifiable homicide! But I'm not going to kill you, Hilly. That would be too sweet. I'm not going to do one damned thing to you ever again, except divorce you. You can just lie here and rot like the dog meat you are. You are selfish to the bottom of your soul. Now you can lie here all by your own sweet self, the only person in the world you've ever loved. You've got years to enjoy your famous bedside manner. I'm taking your money and your children, and I'm going someplace hot where the men have young, strong cocks that stand up straight. So long, Hilly. I'll think of you from time to time while I'm getting laid on an island somewhere. And I know you'll be thinking about me. You haven't got another blessed thing to do. You'll be hearing from my divorce lawyer, sweetheart. Remember him? If he's half as good a lawyer as he is a lover, you're in deep shit, Hilly."

❂ ❂ ❂

"Man, that woman has got a mouth!" said Mr. Devereux. "You never told me, Doctah Sunshine, what a Rabelaisian *mouth* your woman has. Poor Doctah. You must be feelin' pretty bad right now, but you'll feel better after a while. I know you will. She had a pretty bad shock. She's hurtin', you know. They all act like that at first. But she'll calm down. After a while she'll get to rememberin' sweeter times. And the kids'll want their daddy. And the old guys she'll meet at her age won't be able to get it up, *hee-hee*. And I don't think she'll have enough money to buy her a young one. Not for very long, anyhow. You'll see. She'll figure it all out. Then she'll be back. All lovey like she was yesterday. Meantime, I don't care if I say it out loud—Clarinet and I won't mind the quiet."

48 SATURDAY, JUNE 17, 1978
3:13 A.M. HERRICK HOSPITAL I.C.U.

From his hospital bed, Dr. Sunshine recalled that on Monday, March 21, 1977, he had come full circle round the zodiac. In one year he had loved "every woman under the sun." Mission accomplished. And his wife (at the time) was none the wiser! Thanking his lucky stars, he resigned from the Berkeley chapter of the International Brotherhood of Lechers. Eagerly, he rejoined Gloria in monogamy and swore, with a Virgo's fierce determination, never to stray again.

Farewell to philandering! Adios to adultery! Auf Wiedersehen to womanizing! Ciao to cheating! For the time being.

During his Zodiac Tour, he had deviated only once from his master plan. One February evening after work, before making an astrological house call on his Pisces, he stopped by Sam Horowitz's office to return a psychiatric textbook he had borrowed. Dr. Horowitz, it turned out, had left early for a meeting, but his young, fair-haired wife, who served as his secretary, was still in the office.

His fingers grazed hers as he handed her the book. Not unacquainted with the legendary Dr. Sunshine's exploits—she had been watching his discarded women troop by for months—she looked up at his smiling face and said, "I can see why women fall for you."

At the urging of Poindexter, Dr. Sunshine temporarily abandoned astrology to embrace psychiatry. Throwing caution, friendship, and two Commandments to the winds, he led her to her husband's couch.

After this one departure from his grand design, Dr. Sunshine resumed his celestial mission, oblivious to the fact that he had just screen-tested for an assassination.

49 FRIDAY, JUNE 23, 1978
8:00 A.M. HERRICK HOSPITAL I.C.U.

After three months in I.C.U., Dr. Sunshine was still neurologically locked-in. The progress notes dutifully inscribed by his doctors in his chart had long since become a two-word exercise in penmanship: "Status quo." "Status quo." "Status quo."

Dr. Sunshine could see, but could only move his eyes up and down. He could signal "yes" and "no" by blinking once or twice. He could hear and smell. He could not speak, swallow, move, or feel his nurses' touches, pats, or caresses. He felt no pain, just numbness—the most disturbing of his physical afflictions. He had a keen nostalgia for food and sex, but lacking a sensate body, no real appetite for them. Throughout Dr. Sunshine's ordeal, Poindexter remained stiffly at attention, like a rifleman guarding the Tomb of the Unknown Soldier.

Dr. Sunshine could think and therefore, according to Descartes, he was. Was what? For all practical purposes, a lovingly cared-for indoor plant inside a clean, well-lighted greenhouse.

Copiously, three times a day, the nurses recorded in his chart their observations of his hospital existence: blood pressure, pulse rate, respirations, temperature, size of pupils, condition of skin, rhythm of heart, level of consciousness, fluids in, fluids out, medications given. They had no way to record the extent of his greatest affliction—his agony over losing his wife and children.

One morning, while propped up on his side, he caught sight of his chart in the hands of one of his surgeons. The chart bulged ominously—like a poisoned pup—as had the charts of his own patients shortly before they died.

In that bright, sunless, moonless room, Dr. Sunshine could tell the time of day by the change in the cast of characters on each nursing shift. Seven to three were the beautiful single nurses, three to eleven were the tired, married nurses, and eleven to seven were the wacko nurses. He loved them all, and they, in turn, constantly visited his bedside, cleansing the very air about him with their compassion.

The radio also gave him the time of day and night, but in that room of perpetual fluorescence, such words as "9:00 A.M." did not have any meaning in his reality. What the radio told him of the passage of time was that string quartets meant the sun had risen, the big, meat-and-potatoes orchestral works meant the sun was overhead, and the atonal blips, whines, and crashes of the twentieth-century electronic composers meant the sun had set—if not outside, then certainly on the world of music as he had known and loved it.

Using a mixed bag of mantras and mandalas recalled from his extensive browsing at the Eastern Eye bookstore, Dr. Sunshine meditated for twenty minutes each eight-hour shift—twenty semi-blissful minutes of retreat from the battlefield of his body.

Then, for one hour each shift, he silently played General Patton to his weary phagocytes:

"O.K., UP AND AT 'EM! MOP UP THAT SPINAL CORD! SURROUND THOSE BACTERIA, YOU COCCI-SUCKERS! WHATSA MATTER? YOU WANNA LIVE FOREVER?"

The rest of the time he ruminated.

He thought of all the things he would be well rid of when he died: trucks, dentists ("God, deliver me from dentists with toothbrush mustaches!"), mildewed towels, medical insurance forms, lawyers, his office telephone ("Dr. Sunshine, Mrs. Rifkin is crying in pain on line two and her nephew, Dr. Seymour Rifkin of Chicago, is holding on line three"). That was all.

The rest of life he would miss terribly: Gloria, Jonathan, Michael, anchovies, women, chamber music, clear orange Jell-O, internal medicine, backlit flowers, steak tartare, autumn leaves, champagne, bookstores, dark-chocolate mousse . . .

At 4:10 P.M. on June 26, 1978, a News Brief on the radio interrupted Dr. Sunshine's reverie. The baritone announcer reported,

"In Oakland, the trial of twelve women suspected in the assassination attempt on Berkeley internist Dr. Hillel Sunshine got underway today with efforts to select a jury. Chained at the ankles and wrists, the twelve defendants looked on impassively while their attorney, the legendary Paxton ("The Spider") Webb of San Francisco, challenged the first sixty-three prospective jurors.

"Observers predicted at least two weeks would be required for the selection of the jury to sit in judgment on the 'Doctor's Dozen,' as the defendants have come to be called . . . "

Dr. Sunshine looked up to see Devereux and Clarinet staring down at him anxiously.

"Those bitches," said Clarinet. Devereux nodded emphatically.

Dr. Sunshine gazed blankly at the two men, but Poindexter reacted dramatically. He suddenly lost his rigidity, collapsing the little tent he had made of the bed sheet. Devereux and Clarinet instantly recognized this as the first promising neurologic sign the patient had shown since his admission to the hospital. Clarinet lifted up a corner of the bedsheet, peeked in, and announced, "Thank God—he's resting comfortably at last."

The shock of hearing his name over the radio, and the news of the impending trial, had squirted seventy milligrams of hydrocortisone from Dr. Sunshine's adrenal cortex into his blood stream. This bolus of corticosteroid suddenly facilitated neurotransmission across 1,803 damaged synapses in the doctor's spinal cord. Poindexter finally received sufficient inhibitory stimuli to go limp.

Dr. Sunshine looked down at the flattened sheet and began weeping. Mr. Clarinet dried his tears. It was the first time Dr. Sunshine had ever felt overjoyed at losing an erection.

50 MONDAY, JULY 9, 1978 9:00 A.M. ALAMEDA COUNTY COURTHOUSE, OAKLAND

The dirty secret to Paxton ("The Spider") Webb's fabled success as a defense attorney lay in his uncanny ability to size up a prospective juror. Often as not, by the time a trial got under way, he had, as he put it, "Four jurors in my pocket, three eating out of my hand, and the last five willing to kill for me."

His jury selection for the Doctor's Dozen trial was his masterpiece: twelve overweight, middle-aged divorcées, once obviously attractive, now among the walking wounded in the battle of the sexes— twelve women united in their hatred of errant husbands.

As he stood before these twelve angry women, he could taste victory. His defense of the Doctor's Dozen, who had been victimized by a philanderer, would be a piece of cake.

On the opening day of the trial, The Spider used to full advantage his tall, athletic build, his silver, widow's-peaked hair, his deep Texas tan, his bugle-charge voice, his black Brioni suit, and his red silk tie. He mesmerized judge, jury, prosecutors, spectators, and the press. With the possible exception of Lenny Bruce in his heyday, no one ever worked a room better than The Spider did in the first weeks of the Doctor's Dozen trial.

"Ms. Lustbender, would you kindly tell the gentlewomen of the jury precisely how you felt when Dr. Sunshine jilted you and then referred you to a psychiatrist?

"Used! Insulted! Betrayed!"

"I see. And did the psychiatrist—the late Dr. Horowitz—encourage you to act out your feelings toward Dr. Sunshine?"

"Yes, he told me to kill the bastard."

By the time Judge Tickner recessed the court on the fifth day of the trial, The Spider found himself figuratively clasped to the bosoms of the hefty jurors as tightly as their bras.

51 WEDNESDAY, AUGUST 9, 1978 12:00 NOON. HERRICK HOSPITAL I.C.U.

Shortly after Poindexter's celebrated fall, Dr. Sunshine began experimenting with the dangerous meditative technique of astral travel, an out-of-body experience about which he had studied intently one rainy afternoon in the Eastern Eye bookstore. Those claiming to have succeeded at astral travel reported that there was actually a second, ephemeral body, made of a fine, light material, which separated from one's physical body, but remained connected to it by a thread. Dr. Sunshine would have given his soul to be in that courtroom and he felt he owed it to himself to make at least, as he termed it, a half-astral try.

The lack of distractions from his numbed body greatly enhanced his ability to concentrate. After six weeks of strenuous effort, he succeeded.

At 12:10 P.M. on the afternoon of August 9, 1978, he looked up to see the gossamer image of a Jewish internist begin to extrude from his navel. As he watched the ectoplasm taking shape, he experienced the thrill of a mother giving birth, of a prisoner breaking out, of an outraged angel ascending to his revenge.

The sensational trial was well under way by now. Defense counsel Paxton ("The Spider") Webb was weaving a brilliant case of collective insanity to account for his defendants' "admittedly bizarre reprisal against the satanic Dr. Sunshine."

Attached to an even finer thread than that spun by The Spider, the ectoplasmic shell of Dr. Sunshine, wearing a white hospital gown, wafted unobtrusively through the open door of Department Ten of the Alameda County Courthouse during afternoon recess on the forty-third day of the trial.

When Judge Harold Tickner gaveled the court to order at 1:00 P.M., the wraith of Dr. Sunshine stood undetected just behind a sheriff's deputy at the back of the large, jam-packed room.

An assistant district attorney, replacing the one The Spider had had for breakfast, stood up to cross-examine defendant number one, a redhead.

"Ms. Lustbender, would you have the members of the jury believe that Dr. Sunshine was a heartless seducer—'a monster,' I believe you called him—who robbed you of your self-respect and gave you nothing, absolutely *nothing*, in return? Not even one gift?"

"I object, your Honor," said The Spider. "Counsel is just harassing this witness."

"I don't think he is," said Judge Tickner with an uncharacteristic twinkle in his eye. "Please answer the question, Ms. Lustbender."

"Besides a few cheesy trinkets, he gave me *nothing*," said the defendant, in a low, even voice. "That bastard was so tight you could feed him quarters and he'd shit nickels."

"Order in the courtroom," gaveled the judge.

"Thank you, Ms. Lustbender," said the assistant district attorney, turning to the bench. "Your Honor, I would like to submit into evidence a plumbing bill made out to Ms. Valerie Lustbender and stamped, 'Paid in Full.'"

When the plumbing bill, designated Prosecution Exhibit #87, had been duly entered, the assistant district attorney asked, "Is it not true, Ms. Lustbender, that Dr. Sunshine had installed, at his own expense, a portable Jacuzzi in your residential bathtub?"

"He never gave me any Jacuzzi," she snapped, darting a glance at The Spider.

"Ms. Lustbender, I just had submitted into evidence a bill for a portable Jacuzzi made out to your name and paid for in full by Dr. Sunshine. His canceled checks for 1976 and 1977, previously submitted in evidence, include one made out to Gorham Plumbing on April 5, 1976 for the exact amount on the statement in question."

Through clenched teeth, she repeated, "He never gave me any Jacuzzi."

At this point, a semitransparent apparition in a wrinkled white gown suddenly materialized halfway down the center aisle of the courtroom. The ghost of Dr. Sunshine pointed a dead-white finger at the defendant and cried, *"Jacuzzi!"*

As one awed courtroom reporter put it, "Some wacko walked in off the street and created a moment in the history of Common Law that for sheer drama rivaled Zola's immortal pronouncement, *'J'accuse!'* at the time of the Dreyfus trial."

Gaping at her spectral accuser, the defendant promptly fell off the witness stand in a dead faint. Her eleven shackled co-defendants rose en masse, jerked their heads over their left shoulders, then, following their leader, pitched forward in a collective swoon. In their orange jumpsuits, they appeared to another reporter as "a row of golden California poppies felled by a single swipe from the Grim Reaper."

In the ensuing confusion, the judge recessed the court. The vindicated ectoplasm of Dr. Hillel Sunshine flitted Chagall-like over the rooftops of Berkeley to reenter his moribund body in Herrick Hospital.

52 WEDNESDAY, AUGUST 16, 1978
12:30 P.M. HERRICK HOSPITAL I.C.U.

Dr. Sunshine's out-of-body experience was almost his undoing. While his astral being was having its day in court, his corporeal remains were falling apart. It was Mr. Clarinet who signaled the Code Blue on Dr. Sunshine. A team of twelve nurses and doctors labored over his lifeless body for the one-hour duration of his round-trip to the courthouse.

When his ectoplasmic gadabout returned, it shed its gown and hovered over the bed, unwilling to reenter its host's body. His giddy, astral flight to Oakland had been a startling contrast to his solitary confinement of the past five months.

It was with the greatest reluctance that Dr. Sunshine finally reintegrated his spirit and flesh. From his research, he knew that if he had chosen to give up his ghost and abandon his body to the morgue, his ectoplasmic shell would have begun jetting flatulently about the room like a released balloon, diminishing rapidly to nothingness.

The almost-dead body he rejoined, first rallied, then regressed. His doctors' progress notes abruptly changed from the terse "Status quo" to lengthy descriptions of his daily decline.

Within seven days, Dr. Sunshine lost all he had gained in five months. He was back on the ventilator, the artificial kidney, and the cardiac pacemaker. The neurosurgeon ordered an EEG that revealed, if not out-and-out brain death, then the next thing to it.

As he drifted into semicoma, Dr. Sunshine lost his ability to open his eyes, while Poindexter rose ominously beneath the bed sheet.

53 TUESDAY, AUGUST 29, 1978
1:00 P.M. BOARDROOM,
HERRICK HOSPITAL

Dr. Sunshine's former patients had been following his case with morbid fascination and, for the most part, deep compassion. Among the more fascinated was one of his most trying patients, Dr. Samantha

Holly Fairbanks-Klein, a clinical psychologist specializing in death and dying, or "D & D," as she termed her life's work.

Thanks to her counseling, scores of terminally ill Berkeley patients had shuffled blissfully off this mortal coil, ecstatic at not having to look up once more into the frowning, cold-eyed, blankly lovely face of Dr. Samantha Holly Fairbanks-Klein.

As Dr. Sunshine's patient, she had been seeing him for ten years with a variety of morbid psychosomatic complaints, each of which, to her keen disappointment, had proved less than fatal. For the last ten of her forty-eight years she had been training herself to take in perfect stride news of her own imminent demise—news that Dr. Sunshine perversely denied her. In anticipation of that momentous day when he would tell her that she had six months to live, she had rehearsed how she would behave during the Denial stage, the Anger stage, the Depressed stage, and, finally, the Resigned stage. Hers would be a death that would live in the hearts and minds of Berkeley's psychotherapeutic community forever.

In the meantime, as newspaper reports appeared of Dr. Sunshine's latest setback, she could take it no longer. If ever any man deserved to die with dignity, she concluded, it was her good, graying internist, Dr. Sunshine.

An expert in the use of the telephone as a blunt instrument, she phoned each of Dr. Sunshine's physicians one Tuesday afternoon. She announced that she was appointing them members of her ad hoc Ethics Committee to determine if Dr. Sunshine's right to die was being denied. She told them that she had phoned Mrs. Sunshine in Pittsburgh, who had assured her that the sooner her husband died, the better. She warned the doctors that if they refused to meet in committee, she would seek a court injunction—with the aid of her husband, Judge A. Helmut Klein—forcing them to show just cause for continuing life-sustaining procedures on the moribund Dr. Sunshine.

Finally, she had taken the liberty of inviting a representative of Dr. Sunshine's health insurance carrier, Blue Shaft of California, to discuss with the committee the cost-benefit ratio of prolonged intensive care of a comatose patient.

Mr. Devereux, who made a practice of keeping his eyes and ears open, and his mouth shut, overheard three of Dr. Sunshine's physicians discussing the upcoming meeting with Dr. Fairbanks-Klein.

"Ah hate to admit it," said Dr. Levine, the vascular surgeon, "but the bitch may have a point."

"You're right. The poor fellow's had it, I'm afraid," said Dr. Edwards, the neurosurgeon. "Here's a copy of his latest EEG—Oh dear, oh shit, oh dear, just look at that."

"Ssssss," said Dr. Kanamura.

"Fuuuck," said Dr. Levine.

The ad hoc Ethics Committee met in the boardroom on the fifth floor of Herrick Hospital on the afternoon of September 1, 1978. Mr. Devereux pressed a stethoscope against the wall of the men's lavatory adjacent to the boardroom and listened in open-mouthed horror as Dr. Fairbanks-Klein summarized the committee's opinion.

"Now then, the patient's physicians, here in attendance, are in unanimous agreement that Dr. Sunshine is unsalvageable. I wish to thank especially Mr. Groins of Blue Shaft of California for his illuminating comments. Certainly, no one would begrudge the $263,417.43 so far expended on Dr. Sunshine, but I think I speak for all of us in stating that, out of ethical considerations, a further contribution to Dr. Sunshine's high cost of dying would be throwing good money after bad. Mrs. Sunshine, in a phone conversation I took the liberty of recording, states that she emphatically opposes further efforts to sustain Dr. Sunshine's tenuous life.

"So, gentlemen, it's resolved that after ordering a comforting dose of morphine, you will forthwith disengage Dr. Sunshine from all life-support equipment in order to facilitate a speedy, merciful passage of our beloved friend and colleague.

"Also, out of ethical considerations, I strongly urge each of you to write in the patient's chart a detailed account of your clinical appraisal of his hopeless situation before you take any euthanasic measures. Otherwise, we as an ad hoc Ethics Committee, won't have a leg to stand on. If there are no further questions, the meeting is adjourned."

Mr. Devereux heard the committee members shuffle out of the boardroom and head for the fifth-floor elevator. Leaning into the shaft, Mr. Devereux waited, out of ethical considerations, until the elevator had descended to the third floor, before he cut through the main cable with a power saw.

When the elevator came to an abrupt stop in the basement, the Ethics Committee, alas, did not have a leg to stand on. A team of nine orthopedic surgeons stayed up half the night reuniting the fractures of eleven femurs, eight tibias, and thirteen fibulas before the committee members reassembled in adjacent rooms on Herrick Three North.

From her hospital bed, Dr. Samantha Holly Fairbanks-Klein looked down at her two long-leg casts and wondered how long it might take her to develop thrombophlebitis followed by a massive pulmonary embolus.

An expression of infinite sweetness stole over her unlined, alabaster face. She closed her faintly veined eyelids and pressed together the palms of her cool hands over her cold, cold breasts. At peace, she fell asleep, dreaming of Westminster Abbey. Of all those serenely pale marble queens lying supine atop their sarcophagi.

54 WEDNESDAY, AUGUST 30, 1978
8:30 P.M. WANDERLUST INN, OAKLAND

The reality of their being a sequestered jury dawned on the twelve ladies when they checked into Oakland's Wanderlust Inn, the past scene, as yet unknown to them, of one of Dr. Sunshine's unhappier trysts. Under contract with the Alameda County Department of Justice to provide bed and board for sequestered jurors, the Wanderlust was the flagship in a sinking motel enterprise known as Rest-in-the-West, Inc.

Assigned two to a room, the jury members showered their first night in cold, rusty water—their baptism—before dressing for dinner in front of overly lit mirrors—their revelation—and then heading for the dining room—their Gethsemane.

The motel's restaurant was called the Pink Sail. After fifteen years of execrable food and worse service, the Pink Sail now catered exclusively to a clientele of sequestered jurors.

Accompanied by a sad-eyed sheriff's deputy whose droopy mustache and bulky omnipresence they would soon come to loathe, the twelve starved jurors in the Doctor's Dozen trial waddled expectantly into the Pink Sail on the night of July 19, 1978.

It was a large room, obviously built with great expectations. Its gravy-stained, oak-paneled walls were encrusted with nautical kitsch: tarnished brass portholes, graffiti-etched lifesavers, and tattered fishing nets bulging with dusty glass balls. Cracked ship's lanterns gave off a bluish light that flattered each diner with the complexion of an ancient mariner seven days drowned.

The center of the room was dominated by a stout, twenty-foot mizzenmast clearly rigged by drunken sailors during a hurricane. Its once proud, pink sail sagged on its yardarms—a ragtag and bobtail of torn canvas and tangled ropes.

Finding themselves alone in the large room, the jurors seated themselves at one of the many tables set for twelve. Eventually, a middle-aged Filipino waiter, three sheets to the wind, tacked out of the kitchen with an armful of pink, triangular menus and announced, "Cook time almost go home—so you order now, okay?"

Ignoring him, the women disappeared for several minutes behind the huge menus.

"On page two, I count three hundred calories in grease stains alone," remarked a juror.

"Does the 'Captain's Platter' come with clam chowder?" asked another.

"Yes . . . no," said the waiter.

"What do you mean, 'Yes . . . no'?"

"Yes, 'Capeetain Bladder' he come with chowr. No, we got no chowr anymore."

"Is the lobster in the 'Hoof 'n' Claw' fresh?" asked another juror, in a high-pitched New England voice. "And is the steak aged?"

"Whar you min?" the waiter asked, bending over her menu.

"Here," she said, pointing to an area of large print surrounded by a black box. "This obituary notice entitled 'Hoof 'n' Claw' at the top of page three."

"Oh yeah, dat," he said, his eyes threatening to light up with compassion. "We give you var nice deep-fry feesh pats and broil mit pats."

"I'd hate to be pinched by a feesh pat," she said.

"Or trampled by a mit pat," said another. " 'Hoof 'n' Claw' my foot!"

"With the Dover sole," asked another, "do I get a choice of baked potato or french fries?"

"Yes . . . no."

After fifteen minutes of increasingly opaque negotiations with the waiter, a red-faced woman got to her feet and announced, "We're all going to have Number 83, 'Crab Legs Sautéed in Wine Sauce' and *that's all there is to it!*"

"Okay-doke," said the waiter, moistening the tip of his pencil with the tip of his tongue, "all twelve they get Numbre Hate Tree. What you wan' on salads—bloochee or house dress?"

"What's the house dressing?"

"Bloochee."

"Well, in that case, make it six of one, half a dozen of the other."

The waiter's appearance in the kitchen near closing time with twelve orders of crab legs sautéed in wine sauce was greeted by a shrill Cantonese oath from the chef, followed by a terrific din of thrown woks and cleavers. A half hour later, the ashen waiter reappeared, wheeling a large, wobbly metal cart into the dining room. Soon, the famished jurors were tearing into their deep-fried fish patties and broiled meat patties.

"But this is the 'Hoof 'n' Claw'!" protested one of the jurors.

"The way I see it," said the woman who had ordered the crab legs, "the only choice we'll have the next time we eat here is whether we kill the waiter first, or the cook." (This woman would shortly be appointed foreperson of the jury by her peers.)

No one was able to eat more than a fourth of her dinner. As they groaned on their lumpy mattresses that night from a rare combination of heartburn and hunger, they looked ahead to an endless trial—both in the courtroom and in the dining room—and cried themselves into a fitful sleep.

On the sixty-third day of the trial, The Spider, having successfully weathered the Jacuzzi incident, did a double take as he watched the jurors troop in and take their seats. Something was wrong. The way they walked—less bouncy. Their hair—it had lost some of its sheen. Their dresses—their dresses!—hung *loosely* on their bodies. Their *bodies*!

The Spider's deep Texas tan suddenly turned beige. He was losing them. They were starting to slim down and look beautiful—and preoccupied, each threatening to become the only kind of woman he himself lusted after—and lost—shapely, experienced, jaded.

He could not possibly have known that the points he scored from the prosecutors in the courtroom were being lost in a restaurant to Rudolfo the waiter and Mr. Fong, the chef.

The women's anguished protests at mealtime fell on the deaf ears of their guardian, Sheriff's Deputy Elwood Stoat. While the ladies wasted away to a seductive plumpness, Deputy Stoat achieved true corpulence with take-out orders a fellow officer brought him from a nearby McDonald's.

On the evening of the sixty-third day of the trial, the jurors mutinied. While they slumped at their table awaiting the detested arrival of the waiter, their foreperson struggled to her feet.

"Ladies, I think I speak for all of us when I say that I'm sick and tired and can't take it anymore. This trial's likely to go on for six more weeks and I can't last another day.

"I still crave seafood. But I never want to look another fish patty in the eye as long as I live. I'm going to make *one last request* for sautéed crab legs in wine sauce. If they don't come through, I'm going to threaten to kill myself here and now."

She stood up on her chair and then on the table. She reached up and grabbed one of the nylon ropes dangling from the flaccid sail on the mizzenmast. She tied one end of the rope securely around her neck. Deputy Sheriff Stoat temporarily interrupted his repast to regard her with some interest, a french fry dangling limply from his mouth.

"When Rudolfo screws up enough courage to come out like a man and take our order," said the lady with her neck in a noose, "I'm going to tell him he either comes back from the kitchen with sautéed crab legs, or I'm going to jump!"

"Now you're talking!" said the woman with the New England inflection, climbing up on the table and tying one on.

"Hey, wait a minute, you can't do that!" said Deputy Sheriff Stoat, almost choking on his Big Mac.

"Like hell we can't!" chorused the ladies, all of whom clambered up on the table and grabbed ropes.

If the table had been a boat, the jurors would have been guilty of violating two nautical rules: One—never stand up in a boat. Two—if you insist on standing up anyway, never do it together on the same side of the boat.

Although they had lost an average of forty pounds each since they began dining at the Pink Sail, their combined weight was too much for the table. It slowly capsized to port, accompanied by a chorus of screams—a chorus of screams abruptly pinched short. Shoving the remainder of his Big Mac into his mouth, Deputy Stoat ran to the nearest telephone.

In response to his customers' screams, Rudolfo poked his head tentatively out of the kitchen, then sprang into action. For the first time since he had been waiting on them, Rudolfo gave the ladies prompt service. He whipped out his switchblade, cut free each swaying patron, and untied the rope about her neck.

On Thursday morning, August 31, 1978, the day after the unconscious women were rushed to Highland Hospital, the dailies all blossomed with the same headline:

DOCTOR'S DOZEN TRIAL ENDS IN HUNG JURY

Of course, "HANGED," would have been grammatically preferable, but who would want to quibble over syntax when twelve lives hung in the balance?

55 MONDAY, SEPTEMBER 4, 1978
5:20 A.M. HERRICK HOSPITAL I.C.U.

Since his unscheduled courtroom appearance, Dr. Sunshine had slowly fought his way back up through the textbook layers of unconsciousness: coma, semicoma, stupor . . .

Finally, in a semistupor, he readdressed his internal milieu:

"BULLETIN TO ALL FIBROBLASTS: KEEP THE HELL
OUT OF MY CENTRAL NERVOUS SYSTEM! IF YOU WANT
TO SCAR UP MY OTHER WOUNDS, FINE. JUST KEEP
THE FUCK OUT OF MY CNS!"

He was spending almost all the rest of his time longing for his family. Were Gloria, Jonathan, and Michael okay? Would he ever see them again? Late one evening, he beamed an urgent telepathic message toward Pittsburgh. In her mother's bedroom twenty-five hundred miles away, Mrs. Sunshine started awake from a dream of happier times. "Hilly!" she sobbed.

56 WEDNESDAY, MARCH 1, 1979 7:00 P.M. MENDOCINO, CALIFORNIA

After a five-month delay, the brief retrial of the Doctor's Dozen took place in the lovely coastal town of Mendocino in Northern California. The Spider's request for a change of venue had been based on his irrefutable allegation that the local press had not only turned against his twelve clients, but had come to regard their prostrate victim as some sort of hero in a French farce.

The Spider's real reason for retreating to Mendocino, of course, was to escape the pernicious influence of the Pink Sail restaurant on his next set of jurors. Meticulous in his legal research, he had surveyed the California landscape for a judicial seat that sequestered its juries in style.

In Mendocino he discovered the Seal Bark Inn, a redwood masterpiece designed and built by its owner, Matthew Key, a bearded, handsome Mormon in his late thirties. Upon shaking his hand, The Spider was confident that this architect, builder, innkeeper, restaurateur, and dreamer would be catnip to his next set of ladies.

Flanked by two comely secretaries, The Spider supped in the Seal Bark's ocean-view dining room. The velvety, ice-cold vichysoisse and the small dish of fettucine in garlic-butter sauce were, in themselves, enough to convince The Spider that Mendocino was where he should spin his next web.

As the glazed suckling pig was wheeled out of the gleaming kitchen, The Spider's agile mind leaped ahead to the last day of the trial. When the defense rested, he would present to the jury the prone body of the district attorney, who would attempt to make his closing argument around an apple in his mouth.

After polishing off a perfect cherries jubilee, The Spider retired with his two secretaries for a "nuts and bolts session" in his suite. Efficiently, the legal secretaries took down the attorney's briefs, and he, clumsily, theirs.

Once again, the Spider contrived to pack the jury with twelve well-rounded, middle-aged divorcées. On their first night, two charming waitresses promptly served each of the sequestered jurors a perfectly pink rack of lamb, crisp, golden potatoes Lyonnaise, and an infinitely dark chocolate mousse. Twice.

57 FRIDAY, MARCH 23, 1979
3:00 P.M. COURTHOUSE, MENDOCINO

And so it came to pass—by a vote of twelve to nothing—that one year to the day after Dr. Sunshine had come to grief, his attackers were found innocent by reason of insanity and consigned to the State Female Correctional Facility at Santa Josefina for intensive psychiatric treatment. The victorious Spider had never played to a more responsive jury. Daily, their rosy faces were suffused with the moist glow that only prolonged ingestion of clarified butter and pork drippings can impart to one's complexion.

The reason it took the jury three days to deliberate before coming to a verdict was not that they doubted the essential innocence of the Doctor's Dozen, but rather that they had come to cherish the Seal Bark Inn—its unsurpassed food and ambience, and its spellbinding host, Matthew Key, who regaled them nightly as they lounged, sipping their after-dinner drinks, around the huge, copper-hooded fireplace.

For his part, Matthew Key, perhaps in response to the genetic tug of his ancestry, came to love being surrounded by twelve adoring women each night. Truth to tell, when he waved goodbye to the sobbing jurors as they pulled away in a Greyhound bus, his was one of thirteen hearts that simultaneously broke.

58 WEDNESDAY, SEPTEMBER 12, 1979 12:30 P.M. CORRECTIONAL FACILITY, SANTA JOSEFINA, CALIFORNIA

At Santa Josefina, the Doctor's Dozen came under the care of a forty-seven-year-old, burned-out psychiatrist, Dr. Henry Feldspar, whose four disastrous marriages had amply qualified him for his life's work—the care of the criminally insane female.

It was not long before the Doctor's Dozen discovered that one of Dr. Feldspar's hobbies was sadomasochism. The tip-off was their observation that he was the only psychiatrist in their experience whose walls and ceilings were covered in the same leather as his couch.

The women did not have to twist Dr. Feldspar's arm—although he would have liked that—to get him to show off his collection of buggy whips and tire chains. Soon, during their sweaty and noisy group encounters, the bare-chested psychiatrist, between his yelps of pain, began fondly referring to his patients as "my little whipper-snappers." And they, privately, began calling themselves "Feldspar's chain gang."

After six months of intensive therapy, the twelve patients had successfully thrashed out their basic problem of hostility toward men. Happily bruised and battered, Dr. Feldspar had unwittingly saved their souls.

One afternoon, while untying their doctor after a particularly arduous session, the twelve women threatened to expose his unorthodox techniques unless he recommended to his director that they be released from Santa Josefina to outpatient therapy. At the next staff meeting, Dr. Feldspar stood up very slowly and made an eloquent case for the early release of his wards.

One after the other, his colleagues praised Dr. Feldspar for his unstinting efforts in behalf of his twelve patients.

"Frankly, Feldspar," said the director, admiringly, "we don't know what's come over you. Since you've taken on the Doctor's Dozen case, you've become a workaholic—practically chained to your desk!"

Rather becomingly, the director thought, Dr. Feldspar bowed his head and blushed.

That afternoon, the Doctor's Dozen were declared suitably improved to be able to to continue their psychotherapy as outpatients.

The press not having been informed, the Doctor's Dozen, dressed in Levi's and tank tops, marched triumphantly out of Santa Josefina on Wednesday morning, September 12, 1979, and took the noon train to Oakland.

At 4:30 in the afternoon, they trooped into the Ajax Uniform Company on San Pablo Boulevard in Berkeley and emerged a half hour later, attired as nurses. In a phone booth on the corner, one of them, a redhead, looked up the address of Larry's Rod and Gun Shop.

59 WEDNESDAY, SEPTEMBER 12, 1979
2:30 P.M. HERRICK HOSPITAL I.C.U.

The dramatic recovery and rehabilitation of the Doctor's Dozen was in stark contrast to the condition of their victim. On Wednesday, September 12, 1979, Dr. Sunshine quietly observed his forty-fourth birthday. Following his astral courtroom appearance in August, he had improved somewhat, but was still locked-in—immobilized and speechless. On his master's birthday, Poindexter suddenly crumpled again—the only evidence that some neurologic recovery was taking place.

After the rise and fall of the Ethics Committee, orderly Devereux and nurse Clarinet had assumed the lion's share of Dr. Sunshine's care. Occasionally, an Emergency Room doctor would wander up and lamely offer assistance, but there didn't seem to be anything more to do.

It was Mr. Clarinet's idea to call Dr. Lisa Wong into consultation. On the morning of his forty-fourth birthday, Dr. Sunshine was startled awake by the first pain he had felt since his assault. It was a sharp prick in the web between his right thumb and forefinger. He looked up to see bent over his head a beautiful Chinese woman of forty to sixty years, wearing a silk, high-collared, pale-green pants suit. He looked down to see the origin of his pain—a brass-headed needle that the ivory-skinned woman was twirling clockwise in the flesh of his hand.

"Of course!" thought Dr. Sunshine in an ecstasy of pain. "Acupuncture! The Chinese meridian charts—those ancient road maps to wellness! I've been getting nowhere with the Western nervous system. Ever since medical school, I've hated *Gray's Anatomy*—that Book of the Dead! From now on, the *meridians* will be the escape routes for my locked-in brain. Ouch! Oh, you Buddha-blessed woman, thank you. Whatever you're doing, don't stop. *Ouch!*"

"I think you're getting through to him" said Mr. Clarinet to Dr. Wong. "See, he's crying."

Within two hours, Dr. Sunshine was a pincushion. Dozens of acupuncture needles protruded from his hands, feet, face, and trunk. He could feel the stirrings of pain not only where the needles were placed but elsewhere, in scores of places no Western neurologist could explain—his right eye, his left ear lobe, his soft palate, his right great toe, his navel, his—could it be?—yes.

"On behalf of Poindexter, I thank you, Buddha," offered Dr. Sunshine, in silent gratitude.

At the conclusion of his first acupuncture treatment, Dr. Sunshine could at last feel the touch of his bed sheet on his body. He still couldn't move a muscle, but it was a glorious improvement. Dr. Wong promised to return each day.

The nurses took turns massaging Dr. Sunshine, who reveled in the sensation of loving human touch. Although discreetly passed by, Poindexter subliminally informed Dr. Sunshine that he was not entirely unmoved by the experience.

All things considered, it was turning out to be one of the happiest birthdays of Dr. Sunshine's life.

After daydreaming for hours of his family and of home-cooked meals, he dozed off shortly after 9:00 P.M. At 10:46 P.M., twelve women dressed as nurses joined the mainstream of personnel flooding into Herrick Hospital for the 11:00 P.M. graveyard shift.

This was the wacko shift, staffed for the most part by "floaters," freelance R.N.s who did fill-in work at a number of hospitals. To all appearances, the twelve faux nurses looked like standard, glassy-eyed, floating wackos moving swiftly to their assigned stations.

Splitting into two groups of six, half took the elevator to the Intensive Care Unit on the fourth floor, while the other half took the stairs.

60 WEDNESDAY, SEPTEMBER 12, 1979
11:00 P.M. HERRICK HOSPITAL I.C.U.

At 11:00 P.M. on September 12, 1979, the nurse's station in Herrick's I.C.U. was almost deserted. Only the three-to-eleven ward clerk, Ms. Sheryl Clividge, sat before a bank of video screens watching for aberrancies in the cardiac tracings of nine monitored patients. One of them, in Cubicle 7, was Dr. Hillel Sunshine. The three-to-eleven nurses had all locked themselves in the staff room to complete that most onerous of nursing tasks—charting.

Ms. Clividge did not look up from her monitors when a redheaded, white-uniformed woman stepped into the nurse's station. She did look up when the woman said, "Don't move, lady. If you make one sound, I'll slit your throat."

Ms. Clividge stared at the razor-edged shaft of a brand-new Kessler hunting knife.

A somewhat similar confrontation was taking place in the staff room, where another member of the Doctor's Dozen, brandishing a Magnum .307, instructed the three-to-eleven shift to freeze. Yet another white-capped gunslinger easily herded into the staff room all the bona fide eleven-to-seven wackos coming on duty.

While the three shock troops held the I.C.U. staff at bay, each of the nine remaining women disappeared behind the curtain drawn about Dr. Sunshine's bed. The other patients were too preoccupied with their own dwindling mortality to appreciate that anything out of the ordinary was taking place.

One by one, each member of the Doctor's Dozen slipped behind the curtain and, precisely two minutes later, emerged to be replaced by one of her comrades. The three women guarding the staff were then relieved by their colleagues to allow each of them to take brief, but intensive care of the patient.

The whole operation lasted thirty-six minutes, including the time it took the Doctor's Dozen to walk down four flights of stairs, with Ms. Clividge as hostage, to the hospital parking lot. There, they blind-folded the comely ward clerk and tied her to a metal pole bearing the oddly appropriate sign, "FOR DOCTORS ONLY."

The Doctor's Dozen then climbed into their rented VW van and zoomed off to spend the night at the Wanderlust Inn.

As soon as the Doctor's Dozen had fled the I.C.U., the nurses burst from the staff room and dashed to Dr. Sunshine's bedside. The first one to arrive swept back the curtain. All gasped in unison.

Lying uncovered, the doctor's nude body was once again a gory mess: a smear of red from head to toe. In this latest attack, his tracheostomy tube had been wrenched from his neck. His unblinking eyes were opened wide, his penis terminally erect, his mouth unmistakably fixed in *risus sardonicus*, "the grin of death."

"Should we Code him?" asked one of the nurses, pressing her hands against his chest.

"No, let the poor guy alone," said another. "Now that it's finally over, he almost looks happy."

Instinctively, she drew the bedsheet over Dr. Sunshine's face. There wasn't a dry eye at the bedside as they gave the doctor a minute of silent prayer.

At its conclusion, a raspy voice from under the sheet commented, "Thank you—that was very moving." At the sound of this guttural utterance, three of the nurses fainted, and the rest were in no condition to revive them.

They yanked back the sheet and discovered that instead of being covered with blood, the doctor's body was imprinted from head to toe with lipstick.

During their time with him, each of the Doctor's Dozen had whispered, "I'm sorry, Hilly," and expressed her regrets with two minutes of total-body kiss therapy. The acupuncture had restored his sense of touch; his killers' kisses, his ability to speak.

While the nurses gaped, Poindexter stood regally tall. A liquid pearl gleamed atop his scarlet corona.

No wonder the doctor was grinning.

61 WEDNESDAY, SEPTEMBER 12, 1979 11:40 P.M. HERRICK HOSPITAL I.C.U.

Back from the dead, Dr. Sunshine confirmed that he still suffered total paralysis of his arms and legs and told himself he'd worry about that in the morning. At twenty minutes to midnight on his forty-fourth birthday, he dozed off.

He awakened a few minutes later to the plangent sound of a two-hundred-year-old guitar giving forth a sonata by Villa Lobos. Dr. Sunshine opened his eyes and looked up into the mournful, lovely face of his wife. Weeping copiously, Gloria appeared uncommonly thin, long-haired, and more beautiful than ever.

Without missing a chord, she glanced at the clock on the wall of the nurse's station and said, "It's ten of twelve, darling. Happy Birthday."

Slowly, Dr. Sunshine reached up and framed her tear-stained face in his pale, tremulous hands.

"Glory, I love you," he said. "Oh my God, I can move! It's a miracle!"

Shyly, Jonathan and Michael Sunshine, both wearing Pirates baseball caps, stepped forward and embraced their father. For the first time in eighteen months, Mrs. Gloria Sunshine smiled.

62 THURSDAY, SEPTEMBER 27, 1979 2:00 P.M. THE SUNSHINES' MASTER BEDROOM

"But Hilly darling, not now."

"Why not? The kids are still in school."

"That's not the point. You just got home from Herrick fifteen minutes ago. And Mr. Devereux insisted that you take a nap."

"Afterward."

"Hilly, stop it . . . I can just see me calling 911 for your return trip to I.C.U. Let me help you undress and tuck you in."

"Did you say 'tuck'?"

"Now cut it out. We'll have years to make up for lost time."

"Starting now. Sweetheart, please don't help me undress—lately, anything I can do for myself is pure luxury. . . . By the way, Glor, did you explore any, uh, alternatives to your devoted husband while you were back in Pittsburgh?"

"You're damn right I did."

"How many? Who?" Dr. Sunshine felt lightheaded and sat down on the edge of the bed.

"If you must know, just two. Pittsburgh's finest. Your old friend Aaron Gold. And a lawyer named Mickey."

"How far did you go?" he mumbled.

"Aaron and Mickey amounted to a one-night stand and a forty-eight-hour marathon."

"You had a one-nighter with *Aaron* and a *marathon* with this Mickey?"

"Yes. Well, Aaron and I merely finished a boring evening we started sixteen years ago, just before I met you. It was the longest interrupted one-night stand in history. When it was over, he wanted more. I didn't."

"What's with this Mickey?" asked Dr. Sunshine through clenched teeth.

"You know the type, Hilly. He couldn't keep his hands off me. And twenty other women. Please, God, save womankind from a charming man! Hilly, I learned from Aaron and Mickey that you aren't the only prick that was raised in Pittsburgh. Between the two of them, they have five former wives in psychotherapy. And my old girl-friends told me another hundred horror stories. Hilly, I learned a woman can really get hurt out there. At least you stuck around, stayed my partner, stayed a father."

"I trust you took precautions," he said coldly.

"I assure you we spent more time messing around with condoms and diaphragms and gels than we did with each other. Our sex had the magic allure of a tire change and lube job at the corner filling station."

"Oh, sure," said Dr. Sunshine, wiping his pale, wet brow with a handkerchief. "Aaron and Mickey! Glor, you're killing me."

"No, dear, that's what your darling lovers tried to do, remember? How can you possibly be jealous after all the fun you had? But look, I've come back to you. I love you, and after what you've been through, I forgive you. I think I'm going to be able to, not because you deserve it, God knows, but because, uh, I don't know—because we're used to each other, I guess."

"Yes, used to each other," Hilly agreed. "That's it, isn't it? We've got so much history, and now, thank God, we've got a future."

As her husband painfully removed his shirt, she looked at him as if for the first time. "Hilly," she asked, "who are you?"

"Gloria," he said, mournfully, "the truth about me is like an onion. The more layers you peel away, the more you're bound to cry." Indeed, when he pulled off his undershirt, revealing his patchwork of red, jagged scars, Mrs. Sunshine began to weep. Then, slowly, she undressed.

Fifteen minutes later, he flung himself away from her in a fit of self-loathing. "I'm sorry," he said. "Now I know why the Spanish call impotence 'man's first death'. Glory, I wanted so much to please you."

"Baby, what could you expect after I dumped Aaron and Mickey on you? Hilly, tell me the truth for a change—do you love me?"

"Glory, the problem I'm having is that I love you too much."

Cautiously at first, they caressed each other with a love that finally summoned forth the epic lust that had initially brought them together.

Afterwards, engulfed by a fatigue even more sensual than the sex they had just enjoyed, they curled up, spoonstyle, for a nap.

Before dozing off, Hilly remarked, "Now this is what I call a homecoming."

Gloria murmured sleepily, "I even forgive you your puns, my love."

63 TUESDAY, JANUARY 1, 1980
10:00 A.M. MENDOCINO

Only in Berkeley would an unreconstructed Mormon advertise for twelve wives. Only in Berkeley would a newspaper print such an ad. Only in Berkeley would twelve women even consider such an off-the-wall proposal.

On a whim, the infamous Doctor's Dozen answered the ad. They did not have to wait long for a reply.

The secret wedding ceremony, performed by a priest from a splinter Mormon sect, took place in Mendocino, California, at the Seal Bark Inn, owned and operated by the groom, Mr. Matthew Austin Key, formerly of Salt Lake City, Utah. The twelve brides were given away—with enthusiasm—by Dr. Hillel Isaiah Sunshine of Berkeley, California, who, resplendent in a rented tuxedo, marched with a distinguished limp down the aisle, his left arm gently clasped by the radiant Mrs. Sunshine. The Doctor's Dozen (née the Sunshine Girls) wore white.

In attendance were members of two celebrated juries—one stout and merry, the other marked by a lean and hung look—plus Paxton S. Webb, Attorney-at-Law, who had led the Doctor's Dozen through thick and thin.

After the twelve-ring ceremony, Mr. Key kissed the brides with equal vigor and announced, "I'm the happiest man under the sun!"

Serving as ushers were Mr. Wendel A. Clarinet of Berkeley, who tossed unpolished rice at the departing brides, and Mr. Charles Font-Leroy Devereux, formerly of Mobile, Alabama, who threw grits.

Outside the Seal Bark Inn, the lean and hung jury caught the bouquets. As the brides and groom were spirited away in the longest stretch limo on the West Coast, Mrs. Sunshine turned to her pale husband and asked, "Do you envy the bridegroom, darling?"

"Not at all," said Dr. Sunshine, giving his wife a peck on the cheek. "Why do you ask?"

"Because the end of your dickey is sticking out of your fly."

"Oh God," said Dr. Sunshine, fearing that Poindexter had become a member of the wedding. With relief, he stuffed the few inches of starched linen back into his trousers and zipped up. "These damn tuxedos," he said, "I never could get the hang of them. I remember at *our* wedding, I lost two studs."

"Yeah," said Mrs. Sunshine, "you lost two studs and I gained one."

"Darling," said Dr. Sunshine, "please go easy on the sarcasm. Remember, I'm a Recovering Romantic."